Night of the Jungle Cat

Night of the Jungle Cat

ERNEST HERNDON

ZondervanPublishingHouse
Grand Rapids, Michigan

A Division of HarperCollinsPublishers

Night of the Jungle Cat
Copyright © 1994 by Ernest Herndon

Requests for information should be addressed to:
Zondervan Publishing House
Grand Rapids, Michigan 49530

Library of Congress Cataloging-in-Publication Data

Herndon, Ernest.
    Night of the Jungle Cat / Ernest Herndon.
      p.   cm. (Eric Sterling, secret agent)
    Summary: Twelve-year-old wildlife conservation agent Eric Sterling is
sent to Belize to deal with Black Betty, a jaguar suspected of killing cattle.
    ISBN 0-310-38271-8 (paper)
    [1. Jaguar—Fiction. 2. Belize—Fiction. 3. Adventures and
Adventurers—Fiction. 4. Wildlife conservation—Fiction.]
I. Title. II. Series: Herndon, Ernest. Eric Sterling, secret agent.
PZ7.H43185Ni   1994
Fic—dc20   93-44162
                                                         CIP
                                                         AC

Edited by Dave Lambert
Cover design by Jim Connelly
Cover illustration by Jim Connelly
Internal illustrations by Craig Wilson, The Comarck Group

Printed in the United States of America

94 95 96 97 98 99 /❖LP/ 10 9 8 7 6 5 4 3 2 1

For Forest Parker and Maude Elyse

1

I waited.

Here it came! A tiger, charging out of the bushes at incredible speed! My finger tightened on the trigger. *Wham wham!*

Dead tiger.

Whoa! No time to feel proud—here came two more, moving even faster than the first. I fired, swiveled, fired again, missed, squeezed off a shot at the last second—whew! Two dead tigers.

And four more coming! I let loose, machine-gun style, spraying the field with firepower. One by one they went down. I was panting, my heart racing, my palms sweaty.

Oh no! Here came a whole gang—four in the front, four in the rear. I didn't have time to aim, I just fired. They went down—except for Number Eight. I couldn't swing around on him in time. The beast leaped, mouth open, fangs showing! It was on me, too late to shoot—

"Game over" blinked a message on the video machine. The tigers faded as the machine waited for more coins. Slowly, I became aware of the sounds of the video arcade around me—beeps, rattles, shouts of "All right!" or "Oh no!"

"Nice shooting," said a deep voice behind me.

I turned. "Thanks."

He wasn't a big man, despite his voice. Short and skinny, he reminded me of a bird. His hair was wispy brown, his nose long and narrow. He wore a blue shirt, black leather vest, blue jeans, black boots.

"You Eric Sterling?"

"Yes sir."

He flashed a badge without making a show of it. "WSI," he said. Coughing, he reached into his shirt pocket for a pack of cigarettes.

WSI—Wildlife Special Investigations, a secret branch of the CIA. His badge meant we worked for the same agency.

I looked around the arcade. "Where's Miss Spice?" I said. "The person who called this morning said the director would meet me down here."

"I'm acting director—Roger Bugg. Miss Spice is on vacation." He blew smoke over my head.

"Vacation?"

He grinned. "Went to Hawaii for a couple of weeks. She asked me to handle this assignment. Come on."

Uh-oh. Assignments meant travel, work, danger. This was summertime, time for schoolkids like me to take it easy, hang out in video arcades, have fun.

"What kind of assignment?" I said as we went outside to a shiny red and silver pickup truck. The cab smelled of stale tobacco and was cluttered with boxes of bullets, leather belts, holsters, paper targets with black bulls-eyes, headphones.

"You'll find out. First we've got something to do." He cranked the truck, lit another cigarette, opened his window a crack, and pulled into traffic.

"What about Erik K. and Sharon?" I said, referring to my two fellow agents.

Erik K. was thirteen, a year older than me, a black belt in karate. His sister Sharon was my age and a whiz with animals.

People called him Erik K. and me Eric C. because we had the same first name. In fact, we had the same last name, too, except that he spells his S-t-*i*-r-l-i-n-g. Sound weird? It is. Long story.

Mr. Bugg laughed. "Miss Spice said you liked to ask questions. Don't worry. I'll answer them all."

Soon he pulled up in front of a wide brick building. A sign said "National Guard Armory." He cut the motor. "Grab a set of those ear protectors, if you don't mind."

So that's what the headphones were.

Reaching behind the seat, Mr. Bugg pulled out a pair of suitcases. I followed him inside, past a man in uniform at a desk who checked Mr. Bugg's ID. We went down a hall past several offices, down a flight of stairs, and through a door.

Bam! Bam-bam-bam! We were in an indoor firing range. Nothing fancy, just a long room with wooden floors like a remodeled gym. Several men fired handguns at paper targets with human shapes.

"Put those ear protectors on," Mr. Bugg said, doing the same. I eased them over my ears, and the sharp banging of the guns was immediately muffled. We stepped to the head of a lane. "Ever done any shooting?" he said, talking loud to be heard.

"Well, I have a pellet rifle."

He nodded, set the suitcases down, and opened them. One was filled with boxes of bullets and some kind of scope. In the other lay a fancy assault rifle-type thing, broken down into two pieces. Mr. Bugg assembled it expertly. The gun was short, made of steel and black plastic. He handed it to me. "See how this feels."

"Wow. It's light." I put it to my shoulder and sighted down it.

"Hey! Watch it!" A man dropped to the floor, eyeing me angrily. Only then did I realize I had aimed it in his direction.

Mr. Bugg pushed the muzzle toward the targets with the hint of a smile.

"Sorry," I said, flushing with embarrassment at the angry stares I could feel burning into me. "I didn't know it was loaded."

"It's not," Mr. Bugg said. "But always assume it is."

He took the gun from me gently. I was glad he didn't lecture me.

I watched as Mr. Bugg loaded a curved clip with bullets and slid it into the gun. Stepping to the firing line, he aimed and squeezed off several rounds.

"Pick up that spotting scope," he said. "See if I hit anything."

I peered through the scope at the target. There was just one hole, right over the heart. Now I felt embarrassed for Mr. Bugg. Only one hit out of all those shots!

"You only got one," I said.

"We'll go look. Wait till you hear the all clear."

Soon everyone else finished shooting. "Line clear!" an officer said.

I followed Mr. Bugg down the lane to the target. He pointed to the hole. "Sure I just hit once?"

It was a large hole, ragged around the edges. I understood then: He had put every bullet in the same spot!

2

"Wow! Where'd you learn to shoot like that?" I said.

Mr. Bugg smiled as he stapled a sheet of paper over the hole. "I'm a firearms instructor for WSI. I'm supposed to teach *you* how to shoot like that."

Teach *me* how to shoot? My heart jumped. "But why?" I asked as we returned to the firing line.

Other shooters took their places. "Line hot!" an officer called.

"Here," Mr. Bugg said, handing me the gun. "Don't put your finger on the trigger. Just sight down it at the target to get used to it."

As I looked down the barrel, Mr. Bugg put his hands on my shoulders and turned me sideways. "There," he said, adjusting my grip on the gun.

"Tuck that elbow into your side. That's it. Bend the knees a little. Now, make sure the front sight is in the center of the rear sights and level with the top. See what I mean?"

"Yes sir, I think so."

"All right. This is the safety. Push it off with your thumb. Put the sights on the target. Put your finger on the trigger and squeeze gently."

Bam! The gun went off sooner than I expected. I was so surprised I almost dropped it.

Mr. Bugg smiled. "That's all right. It's got a light action. The slightest pressure fires it. Try again."

As my finger tightened, the gun fired again. This time I was ready. "Did I hit anything?" I squinted at the target.

"Go ahead and fire the rest of the rounds. Then we'll see."

I fired several more times, aiming for the heart. I wondered if I was putting them all in the same hole like Mr. Bugg did. I lowered the gun.

"Always put the gun on safety when you're not shooting," he said.

"Line clear!"

We walked to the target. To my surprise, there wasn't a single bullet hole in the heart. Instead I found them in the head, stomach, knee—even the foot.

"I don't get it! I aimed at the heart every time!"

Mr. Bugg chuckled. "That's all right. This is your first time. We've got all week to practice."

13

For the rest of the morning I shot. Mr. Bugg showed me that I had been "snatching" the trigger —jerking the gun when I fired. That's why I missed so badly at first. Once I quit snatching, my shooting improved.

"The secret to being a good shooter is concentration," Mr. Bugg said when we finished. He broke the gun down and packed it up. "You have to learn to block everything out of your mind. It's all mental. You did well for your first day. By the end there you were getting most of them in the chest cavity. Come on, let's grab a hamburger."

Mr. Bugg phoned my mother from a fast-food restaurant and told her where I was and when I'd be home. After a quick lunch, we returned to the armory. This time he led me out back to a grassy area between two tiny buildings.

"This is a skeet range," he said, opening a gun case. The gun he pulled out looked like a normal hunting rifle. "Twelve-gauge shotgun. Different from a rifle. You know why?"

I shook my head. He held up a shotgun shell, a fat red plastic cylinder with a brass base. "A shotgun shell has a lot of pellets in it. When you shoot, they spread out to hit the target."

We put on ear protectors, then he held up a small remote control box. "Now, when I push this button, a clay pigeon will fly out of that low house, and then one will fly out of that tall one."

"Kind of like a video game," I said.

"In a way. Watch." He pushed the button. *Whiz!* A bright orange disk zoomed out of the low shed, crossing in front of us from left to right. A second later one came out of the high house in the opposite direction.

"Here, you do it." He handed me the control box and readied his shotgun. "Pull!"

I pushed the button. *Whiz! Bam! Whiz! Bam!* Both "pigeons" exploded into bits.

"Wow!" I said.

Mr. Bugg showed me how to use the gun and had me take a couple of practice shots, just to get the feel of it. Then he took the control box. "Say 'pull' when you're ready."

I felt confident now. After all, moving targets were more my style—like the video tigers. Gun in hands, I stared at the low house. "Pull!"

Whiz! Bam! Whiz! Bam!

The disks soared away, untouched. I couldn't believe it! I'd missed both!

Mr. Bugg chuckled. "Not as easy as it looks, is it?"

I frowned. "Why do I have to learn to use a shotgun? You already showed me how to shoot a rifle."

"You'll need to know everything you can for this assignment."

"What *is* the assignment?"

"Let me put it this way. Your target is going to be a lot more dangerous than clay pigeons—or video tigers."

3

After I had fired about a thousand shotgun shells
—or it felt like a thousand, anyway—we drove to
WSI headquarters downtown. We went up the eleva-
tor and into the familiar offices where phones beeped
and computers bleeped. Mr. Bugg led the way into
Miss Spice's large office. He sat in the chair behind
her desk and I took a seat in front.

He gathered up some papers, getting right down
to business, and I found myself thinking, *I miss Miss
Spice—at least she'd have offered me something good to
eat first.* And there was another reason I missed her,
too: She worried about my safety, and I knew she'd
do everything she could to protect me. I didn't
know whether I could trust Mr. Bugg in the same

way. The assignment, whatever it was, sounded pretty scary.

Opening a drawer, he pulled out several newspapers and handed them to me.

"'The Belize Times,'" I said, reading the banner.

"Know where Belize is?"

"Uh—I made a C in geography." C-minus, actually.

Mr. Bugg shook his head. "Kids these days." Rising, he stepped to Miss Spice's wall map of the world. "It's right below Mexico on the east coast of Central America." He pointed to a small yellow strip. "It's the only country in Central America with English as an official language."

"Boy, it's little!" I said.

He nodded. "About the size of Vermont." He sat back down. "Now take a look at the lead stories in those papers."

"Farmers outraged as jaguar mauls cattle," blared one headline. "Mystery cat continues attacks ... 'Black Betty' eludes hunters ... Residents up in arms over killer predator ... Farmers declare war on black jaguar ..."

I set the papers back on his desk. "Does this have something to do with my assignment?" I asked, scooting down in my seat and putting my hands in my pockets.

Mr. Bugg nodded. "Your mission is simple. Kill the jaguar."

I sat up quick. "Excuse me?"

"Kill the jaguar."

Now I *really* missed Miss Spice. "I thought WSI was supposed to protect wild animals—not kill them."

He picked up a newspaper. "I guess you didn't read this paragraph. 'Because of alarm over the killer cat, government officials say they may not follow through on their plans to create a jaguar refuge. Even though scientists say the big felines need to be protected, angry farmers claim jaguars are a menace to the cattle industry. "Why spend government money on a jaguar preserve? Jaguars are our enemy," declared one farmer.'"

"I thought jaguars were like endangered or something," I said.

Mr. Bugg nodded. "Belize is one of their last strongholds. The government was planning to set aside a big chunk of land as a jaguar preserve—a place where the cats could live without bothering people and without being bothered. But now, because of this one killer cat, the plans are in danger. If something doesn't stop these cattle killings soon, the whole country will turn against jaguars—maybe even try to wipe them out."

"Still—do we really have to kill it?"

"Oh, I guess we could tranquilize it, fly it to the States and put it in a zoo or something. But you're talking lots of time and money. We're over budget already. Frankly, it would be much easier just to kill it."

So I have to kill an endangered animal, just because WSI is over budget? Kill an animal because it's cheaper and easier than saving it? What kind of wildlife agency is that? "Does Miss Spice know about this?" I asked.

Mr. Bugg looked as if he didn't like my question. He lit a cigarette and puffed nervously. "No, and I'm not going to disturb her on vacation. She left me in charge and I'm making the decisions."

I pointed toward the newspapers. "It sounds like a lot of people are already hunting it, and they're bound to be more experienced than me. Somebody's sure to get it. Why do I have to go?"

"If some hot-shot hunter down there kills it, there'll be pictures in the paper, more headlines—I want to defuse this situation quietly. If the black jaguar just disappears and the cattle killings stop, maybe things will calm down and people will forget about it. Then the government can go ahead and establish the preserve."

"But why not send a more experienced agent—a grown-up who knows how to hunt?"

Mr. Bugg snuffed his cigarette in an ashtray and rubbed his temples with his fingertips. "I wish I could, Eric. But it's not like this is the only problem we've got to handle right now." He gestured to a stack of documents in file folders on the desk. "I've got all my experienced agents scattered around the globe on crucial assignments already, and things are heating up in Belize too quickly—I can't wait for someone else. There may be a better solution to this jaguar business, Eric, but I don't believe there's a simpler one. One well-placed shot and the problem is solved."

Miss Spice! Where are you when I need you?

"What you'll do is go to Belize posing as a 4-H exchange student," Mr. Bugg continued. "You'll stay with a farm family at the little town of Burrell Boom. They have a boy sixteen, named Jack—a good hunter. We've checked his background and he seems reliable. At some point you'll need to tell him your real mission. It's okay, we'll need this boy's help. I figure you two together can pull off this mission."

"Wait a minute—the *two* of us together? What about Erik K. and Sharon? Aren't they coming?"

"'Fraid not."

"Why?" I felt a surge of fear. "Miss Spice always sends the three of us."

"I'm sure she does, but I think you can handle this job. Sending three people would cost three times as much, and remember—we're already over budget."

"But I'm not sure I can do it without them. Sharon is an expert with animals! And Erik K. is a black belt."

"That's right, and I'm taking this opportunity to send them to seminars for advanced training. I'm sorry, Eric, but this time you're on your own."

4

Mrs. Stirling, short and merry with curly brown hair and red cheeks, greeted me at the door. "Eric C.! We're just sitting down to supper. Won't you join us?"

"Well . . ." I glimpsed the brightly lit dining room down the hall.

"I'll phone your folks right now. I'm sure they won't mind."

"What's up?" asked brown-haired Erik K., muscular and tan, as I entered the dining room.

"I've got a new assignment," I said, not too cheerfully. "One I've got to do by myself."

"We know," said golden-haired Sharon. "We met Mr. Bugg yesterday and he told us. He didn't give us any details, though."

Mrs. Stirling returned. "He said he was sure you could handle the assignment by yourself, Eric C."

Dr. Stirling, a dark-haired, soft-voiced veterinarian, set a plate for me, and I joined my friends at the table.

"Let's say the blessing," he said, and we all bowed our heads as he prayed. Then we dug in.

Dr. Stirling scooped salad onto his plate from a large bowl. "You mentioned a new assignment," he prompted me.

Dr. and Mrs. Stirling and my parents knew all about WSI, of course. They were all proud we kids had been chosen as agents—but I don't think any of them knew how dangerous it was!

"Yes sir. I'm supposed to go to Belize to kill a jaguar."

"*What?*" everyone said at once.

I nodded. "I couldn't believe it either. But there's a killer cat down there attacking cattle. If we don't stop it, everyone will turn against jaguars, and then the government will drop its plans for a wildlife refuge. At least that's what Mr. Bugg says."

Sharon frowned. "But how could you kill a jaguar, Eric C.?"

I shrugged. "I don't know if I can."

"Jaguars—that sounds cool!" Erik K. said, munching a roll. "They're supposed to be tough."

"But killing it?" Sharon said.

"I asked Mr. Bugg about doing it some other way," I said, "like tranquilizing it or something. He said there isn't time or money for that, and we need to kill it so things will calm down."

"I think I can understand the reasoning," Dr. Stirling said. "It's a shame they can't find some other way, though."

"I'll bet Miss Spice would find another way," Mrs. Stirling said.

"No offense, Eric," Erik K. said, "but how are *you* going to kill a jaguar?"

"Mr. Bugg is teaching me how to shoot. I just spent the whole day shooting an assault rifle and a shotgun. Plus there's a guy down in Belize who's a hunter, and we're supposed to team up."

At the mention of guns, Mrs. Stirling put down her silverware and looked at me, obviously concerned and uneasy. Then she looked at Dr. Stirling for his reaction, but he didn't seem to notice.

"Jaguars are remarkable creatures," he said. "They're the largest cat in North or South America, larger even than the African leopard. They may reach eight feet from nose to tail and weigh up to 250 pounds."

"Wow!" Erik K. said.

"They normally eat deer and other wild animals, but they will eat livestock," Dr. Stirling said. "Sounds like they've got an especially bad one down there."

"Do you have a jaguar at the zoo, Dad?" Sharon asked. Her father was chief veterinarian at the city zoo.

"We did, but it died of old age. Beautiful creature."

"I guess you know that Sharon and Erik K. are going to get some special training," Mrs. Stirling said to me.

"Yes ma'am," I replied. "Mr. Bugg told me."

Erik K. didn't look very happy about it. "I'll have to miss a karate tournament. But, hey—I like to learn new stuff."

"Well, I'm thrilled," Sharon said. "I'll be studying under a professional lion trainer."

"I wish you two were coming with me," I said sadly.

"I'm sorry you have to go alone. But I wouldn't want an assignment like that," Sharon said.

"Me either," Erik K. said. "But I'd love to see a jaguar in the wild. Awesome!"

"It sounds like a serious assignment," said Dr. Stirling. Now he seemed concerned and thoughtful. "I hope you're careful, Eric C.—very careful."

5

The flight to Belize only took a few hours. Mr. Maxwell, my host, picked me up at the tiny airport. As we loaded my bags into his dirty tan Land Rover, I found myself breaking into a sweat.

"Sure is hot," I said, wiping my forehead.

"Always like that down here in the tropics. You get used to it."

Soon we were speeding down a two-lane highway lined with shacks—tiny, rundown houses with rusty metal roofs.

"Do people live there?" I asked.

"This is a poor country, Eric," said Mr. Maxwell, a big, beefy, red-faced man who wore khaki clothes and a straw hat. "But things are slowly improving."

We passed a range of rocky hills on the left which made me think of elephants. To the right stretched flat land choked with deep grass and bushes.

"So you want to learn about farming," Mr. Maxwell said.

"Yes sir," I said, playing the 4-H student.

He nodded. "That's good. Seems like every time I'm in the States, all kids want to do is play those video games."

I grinned nervously. "I know what you mean."

"Ever done any farming?"

"I'm kind of a beginner." One time for science class I had to put a potato in a glass of water and watch it sprout, but I didn't figure that counted.

"I've got eight thousand acres. Most of it's still bush. I came down here from Iowa five years ago and bought land up cheap. Then I moved my family down and all my equipment. Started out in sugar cane, but a friend told me there's a big demand for cucumbers, so I switched over."

"Cucumbers! I thought you'd be growing mangoes or something."

He laughed. "There's a mango tree here and there, but Belize is mostly farm country these days, especially northern Belize, and the climate is perfect for cucumbers."

"Are there many cattle farmers?"

"Mostly small operations," he said, nodding. "But there are all kinds of problems: ticks, diseases, floods."

"Are there any, uh, predators?"

He shot a curious glance at me. "Been reading the papers?"

"Yes sir."

"Then I guess you know about Black Betty."

He turned right onto a road that was mostly pot-holes full of muddy water. It must have rained earlier. Right now the sun was beating down. The land was flat and marshy-looking. A few skinny cattle stood here and there in the shade of scrawny trees.

"She's a tough one," Mr. Maxwell went on. "Black jaguar. Cattle killer." He shook his head. "There's something weird about her. Jaguars are known to take a cow now and then, but this cat will kill one or even two a night! She's got an evil streak to her."

As he swerved to miss potholes, I gripped the armrest to hold on.

"There's Burrell Boom up ahead," Mr. Maxwell said.

We passed a red brick schoolhouse, deserted, and I saw a tiny post office with a flagpole, a church with a steeple, and a few rundown shops.

"This sure isn't the way I pictured Central America," I said.

He chuckled. "Belize used to be a British colony, you know. Later it was settled by farmers like me. It doesn't have much in common with Latin America, if that's what you mean."

He pulled to the curb and cut the engine. "Come on, we need to do a little shopping."

We walked into a small store whose door stood open. Inside it was dark and quiet. A black-haired teenaged girl sat behind the counter chewing gum and reading a magazine. The place reminded me of an old country store, full of garden tools, pots and pans, work clothes, and canned food.

"Hello, Mr. Maxwell," the girl said.

"Hi, Leslie. I need some rubber boots for this young man. Plus a hat." He turned to me. "This is mud country. And the sun down here will fry your brains."

We picked out a pair of boots to fit. Then I chose a straw cowboy hat. I took off my tennis shoes, put on the boots, and replaced my baseball cap with the hat.

"Gee, thanks!" I said as Mr. Maxwell paid Leslie.

He smiled. "I expect you'll earn them."

Back in the Land Rover, we turned onto a road even narrower and bumpier than the last. A few miles out of town, Mr. Maxwell turned right into a long driveway full of puddles. He drove around behind a white farmhouse and stopped. "Home sweet home."

As we stepped out, I heard a motor chugging nearby. "What's that?" I asked.

"That's the generator," Mr. Maxwell explained. "We don't have electricity out here, so we make our own."

We walked to the house and went through the back door into a hot kitchen that smelled of vinegar.

"Why, hello!" A short, wide woman greeted me, wiping her hands on a dish towel. "So you're the visitor. I'm Martha Maxwell. Glad to meet you. Robin! Sally! The new boy's here!" She motioned to a steaming pot on the stove. "I'm pickling some okra."

"Martha's a pickle expert," Mr. Maxwell said proudly.

"You have to be, on a cucumber farm," she said, grinning.

A little girl, maybe five, came skidding into the room in her stocking feet. She stopped suddenly and looked down shyly.

"This is Sally," said Mrs. Maxwell. "Sally, can't you say hi?"

"Hi," the girl squeaked.

"Hi, Sally," I said. "I'm Eric."

Then another girl appeared, my age. She had dark brown hair, dark eyes, and fair skin. She wore crisp jeans, tennis shoes, and a short-sleeved white blouse. She gave me a bright smile. "Hi. I'm Robin."

"Uh, I'm Eric. Eric Sterling."

"Glad to meet you."

"Robin," said Mr. Maxwell, "why don't you show Eric around the place? I've got some work to do." He turned to me. "Jack's out in the fields. You'll meet him later."

"Jack's my cousin," Robin explained. "He's sixteen. He's down here helping Daddy with the farm. Come on, we'll put your bags up and I'll show you around."

6

I stashed my bags in the guest room and joined Robin on the back porch, where she was pulling on a pair of rubber boots. She had tied her hair in a ponytail and clamped a ragged straw hat on her head. She grabbed a small machete leaning against the wall. "Ready?"

"Sure!"

Robin led me across the backyard to a path that passed through tall weeds. She expertly lopped them out of our way with her knife as we walked.

"Weeds here grow back as fast as you cut them," she said.

We came to a huge field covered with sprawling green vines. "Cucumbers," she said, pointing with her bush knife.

"Wow! That's a lot. Is it hard work?"

"At picking time it is. Then everybody works. We hire local people to help. Have you ever picked cukes? I have to wear gloves because they're itchy. I don't know, cucumbers are really boring, don't you think?"

I laughed. "I guess. I don't know much about them."

"Maybe you'll be around at picking time. We'll start in a few weeks."

She led me along the edge of the field, our boots sinking in the mud. I was glad Mr. Maxwell had bought me a pair.

A movement made me glance past Robin to the barbed wire fence beside her. The sight made my blood freeze. A snake lay stretched on a limb above the fence, its head inches away from Robin's shoulder. Without time to think, I grabbed her and pulled.

My boots lodged in the muck and we both toppled to the ground.

"What are you doing!" she shouted angrily. "I could have cut myself."

"Look," I said in a whispery voice.

Robin followed my gaze to the fence, and gasped. In a flash she leaped to her feet and struck with the machete, but the wily snake vanished like a shadow.

"That was a fer-de-lance," Robin said, panting as she stared into the dense brush.

33

"Poisonous?" I said, getting to my feet and trying to wipe the mud off my elbows and the seat of my pants.

"Deadly!" She turned and looked at me, wide-eyed. "You may have saved my life."

I shrugged, embarrassed.

"Well—thanks." She glanced down at her muddy clothes. "I don't know how we'll explain this. Maybe Mom won't notice."

"Why not tell her about the snake?"

"Are you crazy? Then she won't let me go walking like this. Hey—come on, I want to show you something. A secret."

"What is it?" I said, following her, surprised she had gotten over her fear so quickly. I was still trembling.

"You'll see." She stopped midway down the field, set her machete down, and nimbly climbed the fence. An overgrown path led into the thick bushes.

"Are you sure we should go in there?" I asked nervously.

"Why not? I've got this," she said, holding up her machete. "Come on."

I climbed over and we set off down the narrow trail, crossing gullies, clambering over logs, fighting through briars. Every moving shadow, every sudden birdcall, made me cringe.

"I haven't been here in a while," Robin said, chopping branches. "Sally's too young to come, and it's no fun by yourself, you know what I mean?"

"Aren't there any other kids around here?"

"A few, but the houses are so far apart I don't get to see them much."

At last she stopped. We were both streaming with sweat. "Down here," Robin said, pointing down a steep bank. We slid down, and at the bottom I saw a small cave tucked into the side.

"It doesn't go anywhere," she said. "But it's a fun place to hide."

She dropped to her knees and crawled inside. I followed. The cave went in about fifteen feet and stopped, its dirt ceiling just high enough for us to sit up.

"This is neat," I said, sniffing the damp earth smell. "But why is it a secret?"

She stared at me thoughtfully, then shrugged. "I just like to come here sometimes and think." She lowered her voice. "Once I swiped Mr. Lee's tobacco —he's Daddy's foreman—and a piece of paper and rolled a cigarette. It was yucky!"

I laughed.

"I used to come here with Maria. She was my best friend, an Indian," she said quietly. "But she moved to Belize City and I don't see her any more."

"Any jaguars around here?" I asked.

Robin's eyes searched my face intently, and her tone was sharp. "Why do you want to know?"

I felt like I'd done something wrong, and I wasn't sure how to answer. "Your dad was telling me about the one they call Black Betty. I just wondered—I mean, here we are out in the jungle. Maybe it's not safe."

Robin took a deep breath, then nodded slowly, letting the air out. "Everybody wants to get rid of her. They say she's been killing all the cattle. I don't believe it, though. I don't think she did that."

"What do you mean?"

She stared at me for a long time. "Can you keep a secret?"

"Sure I can."

"Well," she said, patting the ground with both hands, "this very cave used to be Black Betty's den!"

7

"This is a delicious supper, Mrs. Maxwell," I said, diving into roast beef, rice, gravy, peas, sweet potatoes and, yes, pickles.

"Why, thank you, Eric," she said.

"You'll have to eat a lot to catch up with Jack," Mr. Maxwell said. "That boy's got a hollow leg."

Jack grinned, a forkload en route to his mouth. Robin's cousin was tall and red-faced—he had a bad case of acne—with brown hair that stuck out at all angles. He was thin but strong, and did everything in fast motion.

"Aunt Martha sure can cook!" he said in a Southern accent.

"I'm afraid we take it for granted sometimes," Mr. Maxwell said, with a grateful smile.

"Not I," said Mr. Lee. The thin, white-haired foreman sat at the end of the table with a contented look. "I lived too many years on army rations not to appreciate your cooking, Martha."

"Why, thank you too, Mr. Lee."

He shook his empty fork in my direction. "I served twenty years in the British army here, lad, back before independence."

"He means when Belize was a colony," Robin explained. "It was British Honduras back then."

"That's right," the old man said. "Things were different in those days."

"Tell him how you got the scars on your forehead, Mr. Lee," Jack said.

"These?" Mr. Lee leaned forward, pointing to a cluster of scars over his eyebrows. "I got these in 1968. I was walking into a barn to get some equipment when it struck—a python."

Sally's eyes widened.

"Python?" I said.

He nodded. "Chap must have been wrapped around the rafter overhead. I never saw him. He hit like a prizefighter's punch. Bit me right on the forehead."

"I thought pythons squeezed you to death. I didn't know they bit," I said.

"They bite their prey to stun it," Robin said. "Then they wrap around it."

Mr. Lee nodded. "When I came to I looked over and saw the chap slithering across the ground toward me. I got to my feet not a moment too soon. Ran back to barracks for a sidearm. I got back just in time to keep the bugger—excuse me, ma'am—the snake from escaping into the bush. Put a bullet right between his beady black eyes."

"What did he measure, Mr. Lee?" Mrs. Maxwell asked. I guessed from the twinkle in her eye she had heard the story before.

"Four meters, stem to stern."

"That's over twelve feet," Robin whispered.

"And as big around as my leg," Mr. Lee added.

"Wow!" I said.

"If I hadn't come to when I did, well . . ."

Mrs. Maxwell rose. "Robin, help me get dessert." They went into the kitchen and returned with cake and dessert plates.

"Mr. Lee here has had all kinds of adventures," Mr. Maxwell said.

"Oh, bosh." The old man chuckled bashfully. "Of course, there was the time—"

"Excuse me, Mr. Lee, but who wants cake?" Mrs. Maxwell said.

"I do! I do!" Sally said. The rest of us agreed.

Mrs. Maxwell cut the cake and Robin passed the plates around.

"How long you going to be here, Eric?" Jack asked me.

"I'm not sure."

"Like to hunt?"

"Uh, I guess."

"Going tonight, Jack?" Mr. Maxwell asked him.

"Yes sir. I forgot to tell you—Eduardo saw a track today, not far from the river."

"What kind of track?" Mrs. Maxwell asked, taking her seat as we all began eating dessert.

"Think it was her," Jack mumbled around a mouthful of food.

"Her?"

He nodded. "Black Betty."

"Why can't you leave her alone?" Robin said.

"Are you kidding?" Jack said. "After all the cows she's killed? Besides, jaguar hunting is awesome."

"I think it's a sin," Robin muttered.

"Sin? How can it be a sin?" Jack's already-red face got redder. "People hunted in the Bible. And doesn't it say we have dominion over animals?"

"That doesn't mean we have to kill them all. And the Bible also says we're supposed to be good stewards."

"Enough arguing," Mrs. Maxwell interrupted. "Robin, nowhere in the Bible does it say it's a sin to hunt, but Jack, she's right that we're supposed to be good stewards of God's creation."

Mr. Maxwell put his hand gently on his daughter's arm. "Besides, honey, that cat really has been killing a lot of cattle. And some people around here depend on their cows to survive."

"But nobody has proved that Black Betty did it!" she protested.

"Oh, come on," Jack said. "What do you think is killing the cows, space aliens?"

Nobody laughed.

"Well, what about it, Eric?" He turned to me. "Want to come?"

I felt all eyes on me—especially Robin's. I knew she would be angry if I went. I didn't want to hurt her feelings—but I had a job to do. I looked down. "Sure," I said.

8

It was drizzling and already dark when I joined Jack outside. He wore a baseball cap, and his ragged jeans were stuffed into mud-spattered cowboy boots.

"Come on, we'll take the work truck," he said, leading me to a beat-up dark green pickup lit by the outside porch light.

Jack reached inside and pulled out a spray can. "We need protection from the national bird," he said.

"National bird?"

He grinned. "Mosquito." He sprayed repellent on himself and tossed me the can. I used it and we climbed in.

Heaps of junk—tools, old clothes, spent shotgun shells—littered the floor and seat. A pair of shotguns rested in a gun rack on the back windshield.

Jack cranked the engine in a cough of blue exhaust smoke. The gears groaned as he shifted, and we bucked down the driveway, the dim headlights shining in the misting rain.

"This'll be a good night if the rain holds off," he said. "Ever hunted before?"

"No," I said, holding the armrest as we turned onto the bumpy road.

"I like to coon hunt back in Tennessee. Got some fine dogs. Wish I had 'em here—then I know we'd catch Black Betty. But Eduardo's got some good dogs, even if they are mongrels. I'm a bluetick man myself."

"Bluetick?"

"Best coon dog there is. Some people like treeing walkers, some like redbones. Black-and-tans are a pretty good breed, and I've heard a blackmouth cur is as good as they come. But I'd put my blueticks up against any of 'em. You raised in a city?"

"Yeah."

"Thought so. I'm a country boy. My folks run a dairy farm. I come down here to help out Uncle Bill."

"You like it here?"

He nodded. "It's all right."

He turned down a narrow driveway, tall grass on either side. We splashed through several small mudholes before stopping in front of a rundown shack. The dim light of a lantern shone through the screen door. A teenager stepped out.

Jack cut the motor and got out. "I think we ought to turn the dogs out on that little road near the river, Ed-man. By the way, this is Eric. He's visiting from the States."

The boy, about fifteen, nodded. He was slender, with thick black hair, and dressed in tattered clothes. Like nearly everyone else, he wore rubber boots, a straw hat, and carried a machete.

"Glad to meet you, mon," he said.

"Let's get 'em loaded," Jack said. "She's liable to be on the move."

They loaded three skinny, snuffling dogs into a box in the back of the truck. Eduardo climbed onto the box while Jack and I got back into the crowded cab.

On the road, Jack sped up, shifting rapidly. The truck jolted as he swerved from side to side to miss the worst holes.

"They say anybody in Belize who drives in a straight line is drunk," he said.

We zoomed through Burrell Boom and headed down a long hill. Jack slowed and turned left onto a tiny mud track. He stopped when we came to a long puddle blocking our way and sat studying the mudhole, the truck shaking as the engine idled roughly.

"Can we make it, Ed-man?" he called out the window.

"Keep to de left. I t'ink it will be all right."

Jack eased the truck to the side as we entered the puddle. Water sloshed around the tires, frothy and brown in the headlights. About midway across, the back end of the truck began to slide to the right.

"Keep to de left!" Eduardo shouted—but it was too late. We slid into a deep hole and stopped, bogged down. Jack spun the wheels, which squealed with steam and smoke.

"No good, mon," Eduardo said, climbing down. "Have to winch it out."

"Doggone it!" Jack jumped to the side of the mud-hole.

I watched as the two boys unreeled a cable on the front bumper and hooked it to a small tree by the far end of the puddle. Holding a small control box, Jack turned on the winch. It whined as the cable tightened. The heavy vehicle lurched but held steady. The trunk of the little tree bent and began to crack.

"Stop!" Eduardo said. "Dis tree going to break."

"See if you can find a bigger tree," Jack said.

Eduardo pushed through the weeds by the roadside, then walked farther down the lane. "Mon, I don't see nothing," he called.

"Aw, *man*!" Jack said in disgust. "Might as well get out, Eric. We're stuck—and I do mean stuck!"

9

As I stepped out of the truck I missed my footing and plopped to my knees in the puddle. Cold water promptly filled my rubber boots.

"Oh, great!" I said as I slogged to solid ground.

Jack and Eduardo chuckled. "If you want to bake a cake, you got to break some eggs," Jack said as I emptied my boots and put them back on.

"What do we do now?" I said.

"Let's just turn out here," Jack said. "We can come back later with the tractor and get this out."

"Sounds good," Eduardo said. He opened the box and dogs bounded out, their paws slapping the water.

Jack cut the engine and turned off the lights. He and Eduardo strapped battery-powered lights around their heads.

"Know how to handle a shotgun?" Jack asked me.

"Sure."

"Take that one, on the bottom. It's a single-barrel, have to reload after every shot. There's a box of shells under the seat."

I grabbed the gun and shells, trying to remember everything Mr. Bugg had showed me. I loaded quickly as Jack and Eduardo started down the lane after the dogs. Hurrying to catch up, I fell into step behind them. The hounds disappeared into the bushes, and the two boys stopped and turned off their lights.

The night was pitch black. The drizzle had stopped, and mosquitoes buzzed around our ears. All around, the jungle hummed with a jillion night-creatures.

"Spooky, huh?" Jack said.

"Yeah," I replied.

"Be careful if we get near the river. There's a big crocodile down there, eighteen feet long."

"Yeah," said Eduardo. "I t'ink dat's what happened to old Pepper. I took her hunting one night, never see her again. I t'ink de croc get her."

A dog bayed, off to our left.

"That Belle?" Jack said.

"Yes."

The sound stopped. "Must be cold-trailing," Jack said. "Anyway, they say that croc's only got one eye. Some guy shot it with a .22 rifle. Bullets bounced right off the hide, but one put an eye out. Now it can't hunt too good, so it eats mainly dogs and children."

"Children!" I gasped.

"How many kids has it eaten so far, Eduardo?"

"'Bout a dozen, I t'ink. But none of 'em older dan fourteen."

More howling came from the woods. "Listen!" Jack said.

"Hot trail, mon. Listen to dat pup."

"Come on."

Using his machete, Eduardo hacked a way into the bush. I tried to follow Jack, but as I fought vines, tripped over logs and slipped in mudholes, I wished I had a light of my own.

The jungle opened up at last, but though there was less undergrowth, the ground lay under several inches of water. I wondered if crocodiles lurked here.

Suddenly something seized my leg—something sharp, like teeth. Panicking, I tried to pull away, but the teeth just bit deeper.

"Help! Croc's got me!" I shouted, struggling to get away.

Eduardo appeared at my side, shining his headlight on my leg. "De wait-a-minute vine's got you," he said, freeing my pants from the big thorns. "Come on. Dey got her treed."

Up ahead, the dogs stood on their hind legs with their front paws on a tree trunk, barking excitedly. One dog backed off and threw itself against the tree as if to climb it. Eduardo began to run. Jack was already at the tree, aiming his light into its branches.

"Just a baby," he told us. "See it?"

I made out two eyes, bright green in the light, and saw a small furry body. "That's not a jaguar, is it?" I asked, breathing hard.

"Bobcat. Want it, Ed-man?" Jack asked.

Eduardo laughed, shaking his head. "Dat one still got milk on de beard."

The spotted, bobtailed animal, not much bigger than a housecat, clung to a limb. Its back arched, it snarled and spat at the dogs.

"Come on, let's get these dogs off and try again," Jack said.

Eduardo threaded a rope through their collars and pulled them away. "Get back! Come on, you dogs!"

They didn't want to leave the tree. He dragged them off through the swamp.

Jack clamped a hand to my shoulder. "We're going to get her tonight, Eric. You just wait."

But did I really want to?

10

When Jack and I showed up at the breakfast table next morning, we were yawning and rubbing our eyes.

"How'd the hunting go last night, boys?" Mr. Maxwell asked.

Jack shook his head and gulped some orange juice. "Treed a baby bobcat. Then the dogs took off on something, not sure what. Might have been an ocelot or jaguarundi—some kind of cat, anyway. Must have run ten miles. Never did catch up with it."

"That sounds like a jaguarundi," Mr. Lee said, blowing on the hot tea Mrs. Maxwell made especially for him. "An ocelot would have taken to the trees." He sipped noisily. "Good thing you didn't catch it, I'd say.

"Jaguarundis are scarce these days—ocelots too, for that matter. Not like it was in the old days. I remember when they were both as thick as gulls on Dover. You couldn't raise chickens for all the wildcats."

"No sign of Black Betty, huh?" Mr. Maxwell asked.

"Naw. She gave us the slip—as usual."

I glanced at Robin. Maybe she wouldn't be mad since we hadn't shot the cat. But she didn't look at me, and anger seemed to rise off her like mist from ice cubes.

"We got the truck stuck," Jack said. "Went back and got it out with the tractor when we finished hunting."

Mrs. Maxwell smiled. "Doesn't sound like you boys got much sleep."

I managed a smile. "No ma'am."

"Jack," Mr. Maxwell said. "I need you to run down to Belmopan, pick up some parts for the Land Rover. You can take Eric with you."

"Yes sir."

After breakfast I joined Jack in the pickup truck. "Where's Belmopan?" I asked as we lurched down the road.

"It's the nation's capital," he said, then laughed. "Don't let that fool you. It's just a small town."

A good time to tell Jack about WSI, I decided —but how should I do it? *Hey, Jack—I may have been an absolute klutz out hunting last night, but guess what?*

I'm a secret agent! Or: *Hey, Jack—Do I look like James Bond to you?* I sat and thought for a few miles, and then said, "Jack, what do you think about that jaguar refuge the government wants to start?"

He nodded. "Sounds good to me. If the jaguars have a refuge, there'll be more to hunt."

"I thought you couldn't hunt them in the refuge."

"You can't. But who says they'll all stay in the refuge?"

"What about the cattle farmers? From what I read, they're against the refuge."

"They weren't worried about it until these cattle killings started. Now everything's changed—now some of the farmers want to wipe the jaguars out, and that's crazy. The jaguars were here first."

"Yeah, but you want to kill them too, right?"

"There's a big difference between hunting something and wiping it out. Look, I've been hunting coons in Tennessee all my life, and so did my daddy and my granddaddy. And Grandpa says there's more coons now than there was when he was a boy."

"Then how come so many animal species are becoming extinct?"

"It's not hunting that wipes critters out, it's progress! If a farmer clears a thousand acres of jungle, what do you think'll happen to the animals that live there? And what about all those malls and towns and subdivisions? Naw, hunting don't hurt nothing, Eric. The cats got a chance when you hunt them. I been hunting Black Betty all summer and haven't seen her but once, crossing a road!"

"Why hunt, then, if the odds are so low?"

He laughed. "I just love to hear the dogs run. I grew up listening to hounds. Sweetest music there is."

His explanation seemed too simple to me. But still, he sounded like his heart was in the right place. "Uh, Jack, there's something I've got to tell you."

He swerved to miss a pothole. "Yeah?"

"Well, you might find this hard to believe, but—I work for the U. S. government."

He nodded. "Yeah, you're some kind of 4-H exchange student or something, right?"

"Not exactly. Actually, I work for a special branch of the CIA called WSI, Wildlife Special Investigations. And they want me to make sure Black Betty is killed."

He grinned. "Yeah, right. Me, I'm Batman. Pleased to meet you."

"I know it sounds crazy, but I'm telling you the truth. WSI wants to make sure the government here sets up that jaguar refuge. And Black Betty is making people turn against jaguars—"

"Whoa! Wait a minute, hoss. No offense, but you really expect me to believe a little kid like you is some kind of secret agent?"

I handed him my WSI card. "They have other kids working for them too. They figure we won't draw as much attention as grown-ups."

Steering with one hand, he studied the card, then gave it back. "Looks official, but you could have bought it someplace. Anyway, I don't get it. They want you to *kill* Black Betty?"

"Actually, they want you and me to do it. The catch is—"

"Wait a minute—they want you and *me* to do it? *Me?* How'd the government find out about me?"

I shrugged. "I don't know. They needed a family in Belize that would take a foreign exchange 4-H student and that had a hunter in the house, and they found the Maxwells and you." I grinned. "If it makes you feel any better, they said you were a pretty good hunter."

He drove in silence for a minute or two, thinking it over. Then he said, "Pretty good hunter, huh? Well, they got that right. But I'm not sure I like—"

"Look, Jack, all I know is my assignment, and that's to kill Black Betty, and to do it quietly, no publicity."

He shook his head, puzzled. "What kind of wildlife agency is that? Why would they want us to kill—"

"If the cattle killings stop and if Black Betty just kind of fades out, then people will calm down and the government can go ahead and set up the refuge," I said.

Jack thought for a long time. "Well, I guess it might work."

"Personally, I hate the thought of killing her, but I don't know what else to do," I said. "Plus, those are my orders."

Jack grinned. "Well, Mr. Secret Agent Man, you picked the right partner, that's for sure! I'm gonna get that cat! And if it helps promote the refuge, so much the better."

"I just hope somebody else doesn't get her first," I said gloomily. "Then there'll be headlines, reporters—"

"Don't worry. Most of these folks around here don't know anything about cat-hunting. These farmers just sit on their back porch at night with a flashlight and shoot whenever they see eyes." He laughed. "One old guy even shot his own cow!" Then he scowled. "There is one guy, from Belize City. Claims to be a professional jaguar hunter. He's been in the news a lot. Name's Teddy Fever."

"Teddy Fever?"

He nodded. "Big old fat guy. I saw him one time. If he gets Black Betty, you can be *sure* there'll be lots of publicity."

Jack turned onto the main highway, smooth pavement at last. He grinned again, and reached over and slapped my shoulder. "Don't worry, partner. We'll get that old jaguar—and won't nobody know but us jaybirds!"

And Robin, I thought. *She'll know—and she'll never forgive me.*

11

Belmopan was a medium-sized town full of houses that looked like small gray boxes. The government offices looked like a high-school campus. The streets were all straight and the corners square, like a checkerboard, but palms and flowering trees softened the edges.

We stopped at a store where Jack picked up the auto parts. "Come on," he said as we returned to the truck. "I'll show you the camp."

"Camp?"

He nodded as he drove out of town. "Uncle Bill and Aunt Martha own some land up here in the hills. We come up here and picnic sometimes, swim in the river."

We turned onto a narrow dirt road that twisted and turned between thick stands of forest and stretches of hilly pastureland, very different from the flat, weedy area around Burrell Boom.

Jack paused on a bridge over a small, clear, pretty river. "See that sandbar down there on the right? That's where we swim sometimes. The land is up here on the left." He pulled forward and turned in, stopping at a gate. Behind it rose a grassy slope backed by jungle-covered hills. A big shed—metal roof, no walls—stood on the property among some trees, and several sheep grazed nearby.

"Hey—why the sheep?" I said.

"They help keep the weeds back," Jack explained. "Uncle Bill is just getting this place fixed up."

He turned around and we headed back down the road, through Belmopan, and onto the main highway.

"Hungry?" Jack asked me. "There's a little market up here."

He stopped in a gravel parking lot next to a row of wooden booths under a single tin roof. Half a dozen vehicles were parked in the lot, and people stood at the stalls buying food.

The stalls didn't have much to offer: sandwiches, soft drinks, meat pies, cookies, and some kind of smoked meat. We bought ham sandwiches and drinks.

We were walking back to the truck when a big four-wheel-drive pickup painted in camouflage col-

ors pulled up in a cloud of dust. A fat man dressed in a safari outfit stepped out, along with a pair of helpers in tattered clothes and rubber boots. I noticed a dog box in the back of the truck.

"Teddy Fever!" Jack whispered to me.

The round man pulled off his wide-brimmed hat with spotted fur headband and wiped his sweating forehead. He brushed off his khaki pants, which were stuffed into high leather boots. When he looked up, he noticed Jack's truck with the empty dog box in the back. He glanced at us.

"Well I'll be the queen of England if we don't have a couple of hunters here," he said. His accent sounded faintly British, as if he'd been out of that country a long time. He stuck his pudgy hand out for us to shake. "Teddy Fever's the name. You've probably read about me in the papers." He handed his helpers some money and told them to get something to eat. "What type hunting do you blokes do?"

"Oh, a little of everything and much of nothing," Jack drawled.

"I don't suppose a couple of tykes like you hunt anything as dangerous as jaguars, do you now?"

"Sure we do!" I said, irked at being called a tyke. "Just last night we were nearly on her trail." Jack elbowed me.

"Her? Now who might that be?" Teddy Fever squinted. "Wouldn't be Black Betty, now would it? Where were you hunting, if I might inquire?"

"North of here," Jack mumbled.

Teddy Fever nodded. "Spoken like a true hunter. Well, if you chaps are ever interested in making a few dollars—" He lowered his voice. "I'm willing to pay for any solid information you can give me about the beastie's whereabouts." He patted his wallet. "And if perchance you were actually to kill the furry devil, why, you let old Teddy Fever be the first to know, hear me? You'll be glad you did." He pulled a business card from his shirt pocket and pressed it into Jack's hand. "There's my number and address. Feel free to call me day or night. Now, my stomach beckons. Good hunting, laddies." He waddled toward the food stand.

12

That afternoon Jack went to work on the Land Rover in the barn. He lay under the motor, and I handed him tools when he called for them. I was leaning against the wall daydreaming when Robin showed up. She flinched slightly when she saw me.

"Hi," I said.

"Hi." Her voice sounded squeaky and cold. "Dad told me to find out if Jack was through working on the tractor yet."

"I don't think so." I nodded at Jack's feet, which stuck out from under the tractor. "He's been there a long time."

"Jack?" Robin said. "Jack?"

No answer. Curious, we both leaned in closer —and heard the sound of snoring.

Robin and I looked at each other and started to giggle.

"Are you going to tell your dad?" I whispered.

She shook her head.

"He won't care?"

"I think he just sent me over here to get rid of me. He was trying to work and I was pestering him, I guess."

Her smile faded. Maybe she was remembering to be mad at me.

"Want to go walking?" I said quickly.

She hesitated, then shrugged. "Okay."

We ambled behind the house and down the path toward the cucumber field.

"I didn't tell Jack about the cave," I said. "I really didn't."

"But you did go hunting with him."

"That didn't change anything. He would have gone anyway."

"But what if you had had to shoot Black Betty?"

I had no answer. We crossed the fence and squished along the muddy field. Suddenly Robin stopped.

"That's where we saw the snake," she said, pointing to a limb hanging over the fence.

"Hope it's gone now."

She turned and looked at me. I could see her debating whether to trust me again or not.

"Don't you think it would be wrong to kill Black Betty?" she said.

I started walking again, unable to meet her gaze.

"Let me ask you this," I said. "What if an adult tells you to do something and you feel like it's wrong? Should you do it anyway?"

"Well, the Bible says to honor our father and mother, and it says to respect authority."

"But what if authority is wrong, or you think it is?"

"Hmm. Well, suppose Pilate had ordered Jesus to say he wasn't the Son of God. Would he have done it?"

"No way!"

"Well then." She stopped by the path that led to the cave. "Why are you asking these questions, Eric?"

Again I couldn't answer.

"Come on," Robin said. "I want to show you something."

She vaulted the fence and led me down the rough trail to the cave we'd gone into before. At its mouth, she faced me. "What would you say if I could prove Black Betty isn't the one killing those cows?"

"How could you do that?"

Crouching, Robin crawled into the musky darkness. I followed. "Look!" She held up a small bone in the dim light.

"What is it?" I took it and held it closer to my eyes.

"Deer, I think. And look here—black hair. And paw prints."

The hair stood up on the back of my neck. "Black Betty came back!"

Robin nodded excitedly. "I thought she had left this den for good. Once I started coming here, you know, she didn't come back. But when I came down here this morning, I found all this."

"We'd better get out of here, then," I said, moving toward the light. "She might show up any minute."

"Not while we're here," Robin said, not moving. "She'd hear us talking from a long way off, and stay hidden."

I still didn't feel safe. Wouldn't she protect her den? But I didn't want to leave without Robin. I handed the bone back to her. "So what does this bone mean?" I asked. "And what does it have to do with dead cattle?"

"Don't you see? This is a *deer* bone. If she's eating deer, then she probably isn't killing cattle."

"Maybe she's killing both."

"No! I've read that cats who kill livestock all the time usually do it because they're crippled or sick and can't hunt wild game. But Betty's *hunting* wild game. So she'd have no need to kill cattle."

"Then what's killing the cattle?" I said, sitting cross-legged in the dirt.

She shrugged. "Maybe another jaguar."

"Hey, what about crocodiles? If they kill dogs and children, why not cattle?"

"Children!" She giggled. "You mean like one-eyed eighteen-foot crocodiles?"

"Yeah!"

"Oh, Eric, Jack tells that tall tale to everybody."

I blushed, then laughed. I started to tell her about

one of my earlier assignments involving a thirty-foot lizard, but that would blow my cover as a secret agent.

"So," Robin said, serious again. "Do you think I should show this bone to Jack?"

"What for?"

"So he'll quit hunting Black Betty!"

"I don't think it'll make any difference to him," I said. "You know Jack. He just loves to hunt."

"Oh, he makes me so mad. I mean, he's my cousin, and I do like him sometimes—but why does he have to chase Black Betty all the time?"

"He's not the only one," I said. "That guy Teddy Fever is trying to get her too." I told Robin about meeting him at the market.

She hung her head. "If they kill Black Betty, I'll just die."

"Why is she so important to you?"

"Haven't you ever had a special feeling for something? The first time I found this den, it was by accident. It was late in the afternoon, and I jumped down the bank—and Black Betty was inside. She ran out—and brushed right past me, Eric! She could have killed me, but she didn't. She ran a few steps, then she stopped and looked back—right into my eyes."

Robin's eyes glistened with tears. "Oh, Eric—isn't there anything you can do to keep Jack from killing her?"

13

In bed that night I tossed and turned. What if Robin was right and Black Betty really wasn't killing the cattle? How could I go through with my assignment? I'd be killing her for no reason—or helping Jack do it, and wasn't that just as bad?

If only Erik K. and Sharon were here! They'd know what to do. Being a secret agent was no fun alone.

I thought about phoning Miss Spice, then remembered she was on vacation. And if I called Mr. Bugg, well, I could guess what he'd say: "We're over budget already, Eric. Frankly, it would be easier just to kill it."

And then there was Teddy Fever. I didn't like him at all. Why did he want to be the first to know if we killed the cat? So he could pay us off and claim the credit for himself, that's what Jack figured.

Suppose *I* shot Black Betty—could I look Robin in the eye again? Could I look at myself in the mirror and not feel guilty?

But still, I had a mission. I was a secret agent, and my orders were to kill the jaguar. This was no time to be wishy-washy.

On the other hand—

Someone tapped gently at my door. It opened with a creak. "Eric?" Jack whispered.

"Yeah?"

"Eduardo's found the cat—Black Betty. He saw her down by the river an hour ago. We're going after her. Want to come?"

I sat up, wide awake. "Yes."

"We'll be outside. Hurry."

I dressed quickly and tiptoed through the dark house. The kitchen clock said it was almost midnight. Outside a light rain was falling. Jack and Eduardo stood by the truck with their headlights strapped on, tinkering under the hood.

I heard footsteps behind me—Robin, bundled up in raincoat, jeans, rubber boots and wide-brimmed hat. She carried a small flashlight.

"Are they going after Black Betty?" she asked me.

"Yes."

"I'm going too."

"But—"

"I know I can't stop them, but I can at least be there."

Jack closed the hood and looked up. "Robin? What are you doing out here?"

"Shhh. I'm going with you."

"Are you crazy? Your folks'll pitch a fit."

"Not if they don't know."

"It's too dangerous."

"I know the jungle better than you do, Jack!"

He shook his head. "No way. Forget it."

"Let's make a deal," she said sarcastically. "You take me with you, and I won't say anything to Daddy about the can of snuff I found in the truck."

Eduardo snickered.

"All right," Jack said angrily. "But you and Eric ride in the back."

Robin jumped onto the dog box and took my hand to help me up. Jack and Eduardo hopped into the cab and Jack cranked the engine. Robin and I sat facing the rear, rain peppering our backs as we rode down the driveway. The truck turned onto the road and bounced wildly.

"Hang on!" Robin said. "It's going to be a rough ride."

She took my hand again. I figured she did it just to help us both keep our balance, but it made my heart beat faster.

"What are you going to do if they catch her?" I asked.

"Pray, I guess."

In the box underneath I felt the dogs stirring. Now and then one howled. We passed Burrell Boom, its buildings a misty blur. Then we turned off to the left onto the rutted lane where we got stuck before.

"We're gonna make it this time!" Jack called out the window. "Hold on tight!"

The truck hit the mudhole hard. I bounced off the box, jerked loose from Robin's grip, and was toppling head-first over the side of the truck when Robin grabbed my leg.

"Stop!" she shouted, but Jack didn't hear over the whining gears. As the truck fishtailed crazily, my hat fell off and water splashed my head. Then we came out on the other side and the truck stopped.

"Yee-hah!" Jack shouted as he and Eduardo jumped out.

Eduardo gawked at me hanging upside-down. "What you doin', mon?"

"Oh, just hanging out," I quipped.

Jack came around and stared as Robin pulled me back up. "You two quit goofing off. Come on, Eduardo, show me those tracks."

"Thanks," I said to Robin.

"Sure."

Remembering the snake, I said, "I guess that makes us even."

She smiled. "Who's keeping score?"

"Here!" Eduardo said, pointing at the ground.

Robin and I jumped down as Jack and Eduardo came around to the dog box. I found my hat floating in the puddle.

"We're going to get that cat this time," Jack said. "She came by here not an hour ago, headed straight away from the river. It's going to be tough, though." He looked at his cousin. "Sure you don't want to stay at the truck?"

"I'm sure," she said stubbornly.

The dogs hit the ground snuffling. Jack got two shotguns from the truck and handed one to me. I took it reluctantly and loaded it, afraid to look at Robin.

The hounds disappeared into the thicket, Eduardo following with his machete. Jack went next, then Robin and me. The rain made walking even harder than it had been the previous night. We slipped and slid in the mud and beat our way through soaking-wet bushes.

A dog howled, far off.

"I t'ink dey going to de cucumber field," Eduardo said.

"Doggone it!" Jack said. "If we'd known, we could have driven around there. Ed-man, I think I'll go back and get the truck and meet you."

"Okay. We see you dere."

Jack walked back toward the truck while Eduardo led the way through the bushes and brambles. "I t'ink we going to get dat cat tonight," he told us.

We reached a muddy lane and followed it to the cucumber field. We could hear the dogs baying in the thicket on the far side.

"Dey got her treed, I'm t'inking," Eduardo said.

Robin turned to me quickly and put her lips to my ear. "The den!" she whispered frantically. "They're at the den!"

14

Midway across the muddy, squishy field, Eduardo stopped.

"Listen! Dere's Jack."

I heard a truck rumble to a halt, then a door slam. Soon we saw Jack's headlight bobbing in the darkness. We hurried to meet him.

By the time we joined up at the far end of the field, I was panting. The howling of the dogs in the thicket sounded eerie and loud.

"In here, Ed," Jack said. "Use your machete."

Eduardo hacked a path into the bushes until we struck the trail that led to the den. I expected to find Black Betty hemmed up in the cave, but we passed the steep bank without stopping.

"She must have kept going," I heard Robin whisper.

The dogs were just ahead, baying wildly.

"They've got her treed!" Jack said, plunging ahead. I hurried after him, gripping the cold, wet gun.

"Dere's de tree!" Eduardo said, aiming his light at a short, fat trunk with limbs spread wide.

The dogs barked and lunged. In the branches above them I saw a huge, dark mass. Then the lights picked up two green eyes glowing back at us.

Black Betty!

She screamed. It sounded like a woman being murdered. My blood froze. Jack fumbled with his gun while Eduardo kept his light pinned on the glossy cat, her tail lashing back and forth.

"Shoot, mon, shoot!" Eduardo said.

Jack raised his gun and fired. The branches above the cat exploded harmlessly. Jack struggled to reload. "Shoot, Eric!" he yelled.

Obediently, I lifted my gun. Staring down the barrel, I saw the two eyes blazing like green fire. Suddenly I forgot everything else—Robin, the boys, the dogs. The whole world seemed to fall silent. It was just Black Betty and me. She seemed to be staring straight at me—past my eyes, deeper, down to where I struggled with what to do. I felt the slick curve of the trigger under my finger. I only had to squeeze . . .

The cat leaped. I tried to follow her with the gun but she was gone into the night.

"Are you crazy?" Jack said. "Why didn't you shoot?"

"I, uh—I didn't have time," I stammered.

Confused, the dogs milled around the tree.

"Maybe I wounded it," Jack said, jogging forward to examine the ground where she'd landed.

"No way, mon," Eduardo said. "You missed her clean."

Suddenly the dogs began to bark again.

"Dey've picked up de trail!" Eduardo shouted. "Come on, Jack!"

Quickly, I handed my gun to Eduardo, who didn't have one. "Here, take this," I said, giving him a handful of shells with it.

He grabbed them. "T'anks." He took off after the dogs. Robin and I didn't move.

"Aren't you coming?" Jack asked us.

"We'll walk back to the house," Robin said. "It's not far."

"All right. Don't get lost." He raced after Eduardo and the dogs, whose barking was fading slowly into the distance.

"You sure you know the way back?" I asked Robin, worried suddenly that the two of us were alone in the middle of the rain-soaked jungle with nothing to help us get back to the house but Robin's little flashlight.

She ignored the question. Instead, she said, "Thank you, Eric."

"For what?"

"For not shooting."

"I didn't have time," I said.

"Yes, you did. I was standing right behind you." She leaned forward and kissed me on the cheek.

Whoa! My heart jumped like it wanted to burst out of my chest. *Why do I feel like this?* I wondered. *I failed in my mission to kill the jaguar, but I don't feel like a failure at all. Black Betty's still alive —and I'm glad.*

Then I noticed the distant barking again, and remembered that Jack and Eduardo might get the cat anyway. The hunt wasn't over yet.

15

The next day was Saturday, and I didn't wake up till nearly lunchtime. Robin was sitting in the living room reading a comic book while Sally lay on the floor coloring.

"Good morning," Robin said with a bright smile.

"Good morning." Boy, she looked pretty. *She must be near-sighted to have kissed me, though,* I thought, blushing at the memory. Then I remembered Black Betty. "Did Jack and Eduardo—?"

She shook her head. "I woke Jack up and asked him."

I breathed a sigh of relief.

"Get enough sleep?" Robin asked.

I grinned and nodded. "Did you?"

"Yes. Lunch is about ready. Are you hungry?"

"Am I!"

Jack looked grumpy and tired when we sat down at the table. His mussed hair and red eyes showed that he'd just crawled out of bed.

"My goodness! When did you get in last night?" Mrs. Maxwell asked Jack after little Sally said the blessing.

"Don't know," he mumbled. "After they left—I mean—" He shot a nervous glance at Robin. "After Eric left, the dogs ran Black Betty for a couple hours. We never could catch her again. She headed south."

"Toward Belmopan," Mr. Maxwell said thoughtfully.

"Right," Jack said.

"Toward the hills, I'll bet," Mr. Lee said. "She probably comes out of the hills to kill cattle, then goes back."

Mr. Maxwell nodded. "I read in the paper this morning that another half dozen cattle were killed this week."

"Half dozen!" Mrs. Maxwell said. "My gracious!"

"Where?" Jack asked.

"Around Belmopan, mostly."

"Belmopan?" Robin said. "Then it couldn't have been Black Betty! That's miles from here!"

"I don't know, a jaguar can cover a lot of ground," Mr. Maxwell said.

But Jack looked thoughtful. "Still, though, Uncle Bill. We ran her last night, and Eduardo saw her track the night before that . . ."

"You think it could have been another jaguar killing the cattle?" Mr. Maxwell asked his nephew.

"Don't know. But it doesn't seem likely that Black Betty would have traveled that far—especially on a full stomach."

Mr. Lee nodded. "The lad's got a point. After a cat feeds, it'll lie up for days sometimes. This whole business is beginning to sound fishy. In all my years I've never heard of a jaguar killing a cow every night."

"Maybe it's a whole bunch of jaguars!" piped Sally.

"I think Black Betty is innocent," Robin insisted.

After lunch Jack and I met in his room.

"Do you think WSI will want us to keep hunting Black Betty if she's not the one killing the cattle?" I asked.

Jack shrugged. "You're the one that works for them, not me—how should I know? But this is getting pretty weird, I admit." He lay back on his bed, tossing a football into the air and catching it. "Still, I don't see how it can hurt to go ahead and get her if we can. Even if she's not the one killing all the cattle, everybody thinks she is—so if she turns up dead, they'll all be happy, and then the refuge can move ahead. Right?"

"But that's only true if everybody finds out we've killed her, and my orders were to do it quietly. Besides, what if it *is* some other jaguar killing the cattle, and what if Black Betty's killed and the cattle killings continue—then there'll be even *more* pressure against the refuge."

Jack tossed his football thoughtfully. "May not make much difference what we decide to do, Eric. If we don't shoot Black Betty, Teddy Fever will."

I nodded. "Probably. I think maybe I should call Mr. Bugg. Can I use this phone? I've got a special credit card from WSI."

"Sure, go ahead. He'll agree with me, though."

I put in the call to headquarters. After a long wait, a voice came on the line: "You have reached Branch 521 of the Central Intelligence Agency. No one is in at the time, but if you will leave your name, number . . ."

An *answering machine?* Boy, WSI must be the low-budget branch of the CIA for sure. They must be closed on Saturday. I tried the Stirlings' house. Maybe Erik K. or Sharon would be back by now.

"Hi, you have reached the Stirling residence. If you would like to leave a message . . ."

Not again! I started to hang up, then decided to leave a message.

Beep!

"Hey, Dr. and Mrs. Stirling, this is Eric C.," I said hurriedly. "I'm in Belize and, uh, it looks like this black jaguar may not be the one killing cattle. My instructions were to shoot the cat, but now I don't know what to do. Can you call Mr. Bugg and ask him to call down here and tell me what I should do? This is an emergency because there are other hunters out to get the cat too. I'm afraid she's going to get killed when she's not even the one who's—"

Beep!

16

After church on Sunday the Maxwells began packing a picnic lunch.

"Did you bring swimming trunks, Eric?" Mrs. Maxwell asked me.

"Yes ma'am."

"You might put them on under your clothes. We're going down to our camp in the hills, and the children like to swim in the river there."

Soon we were all crammed in the Land Rover: Mr. and Mrs. Maxwell in the front with Sally in her mother's lap; and in the back, wedged tightly, Mr. Lee, Jack, Robin, and I.

On the hour-long ride, I could see why jaguars were so hard to hunt. Even in pastureland, grass was deep, with plenty of thick bushes. When we entered the hills outside Belmopan, the bushes turned to jungle, just right for a big cat to hide in. Dogs were the only way to locate and run down a jaguar, and even then the wily cats often outsmarted them.

"Here we are," said Mr. Maxwell. Jack jumped out and opened the gate, and we drove up the grassy slope to the high tin shed.

The day was hot and sunny, so Jack and I set up lawn chairs in the shade of a tree. Mr. Maxwell opened a card table, and Robin and Mrs. Maxwell spread the food.

Yum! Fried chicken, potato salad, baked beans, rolls, fruit salad—and of course, homemade pickles. For dessert we had key lime pie, which tasted a lot like lemon icebox dessert.

"Can we go swim now?" Robin asked her mother.

"It's too soon after eating," Mrs. Maxwell replied. "You'll get stomach cramps."

"I read an article that said that's just an old wives' tale," Jack said.

"That may be, but being an old wife myself, I'd feel better if you kids would wait thirty minutes or so," Mrs. Maxwell said.

"Let's play frisbee!" Sally said. She got the plastic disk from the Land Rover and we four kids spread out, tossing it, while the adults dozed in the shade.

Finally Robin said, "It's been half an hour now, Mom. Can we go?"

Her mother smiled. "Okay. Jack, you keep an eye on everyone."

"Yes ma'am."

Jack, Robin, Sally and I headed down the hill to the road, followed it to the bridge, and walked down a path to the big sandbar Jack had shown me.

"Isn't this great?" Robin said as we pulled off our outer clothes. "There's even a swing." She pointed to a rope hanging above the pool with a stick knotted at the end for a handle.

Sally, the first to get undressed, dashed toward the water.

"Careful!" Robin called. "Stay in the shallow part."

Sally splashed out to her knees and plopped down, squealing, "It's cold!"

Jack climbed a leaning tree and, using a pole, pulled the rope in. Grabbing the stick, he swung out, then cannonballed into the water.

Robin went next, and then it was my turn. As I gripped the crosspiece, I felt a nervous flutter in my stomach. I counted to three and launched out. The rope carried me high above the pool. Just before it started to swing back, I let go.

Whoosh! Cold water covered me. I sank in green bubbly darkness. When my feet touched bottom I shoved myself up. I burst to the surface, blowing air. The air felt velvety warm compared to the river.

"Gangway!" Jack shouted, and I paddled rapidly toward shore just before he hit the water.

After several more jumps, I joined Sally, who sat at the edge of the stream collecting pebbles.

"Looky," she said, proudly showing me her pile.

"Cool."

Picking one up, she threw it toward the woods.

"That's good, but watch this." I chose a flat stone and whizzed it across the pool, making it skip. "Try that, Sally."

"I like throwing at the trees better." She tossed another one toward the jungle, then got up to go find it.

Jack appeared beside me. "How many skips can you do?" he asked.

"I don't know. I didn't count."

He flung a rock sidearm, counting as it bounced across the water. "Fourteen! Let's see you top that."

I tried but only got ten skips. Robin joined us. "I bet I can beat you guys," she said. Taking her time to find just the right one, she aimed it carefully and hurled.

"Twenty-one!" she shouted.

"Wow!" I said.

"I can do better," Jack said—but just then we heard a high-pitched scream from the forest.

"It's Sally!" Robin said. But Jack had already dropped his pebble and was racing toward the trees.

17

"It's a dead sheep," Jack said as Robin and I ran up.

The animal lay only a few feet from the path we had walked down to the river on, partly hidden by tall grass. We must have been in such a hurry we hadn't noticed.

Robin put her arms around Sally, who seemed about to cry. "It's okay, honey. The sheep is dead. It's not hurting anymore. Nothing is going to hurt you."

"Must be Black Betty," Jack said grimly.

"How do you know that, Jack?" Robin said.

"She was headed this way, remember?"

"So if it was Black Betty, why didn't she eat it?"

"Maybe something scared her off."

"You don't think she was here when we walked by on our way to the river, do you?" I said, feeling creepy.

"Naw. Sheep's been dead a while. Probably killed last night." He began scanning the ground for paw prints.

"I want Mommy," Sally said, snuffling.

"Come on, honey, we'll go see Mommy," Robin said, taking the girl by the hand. They set off up the path.

"See any tracks?" I asked Jack.

He shook his head. "Something funny about this."

I nodded. "Seems like she would have dragged it to a den or something."

"Well, there's only one way to find out."

"What's that?"

"Get the dogs."

"Will the trail be fresh enough?" I said as we hurried back toward the picnic shed.

"The cat's probably still around here somewhere," he said. "If Uncle Bill says it's okay, when we get home we'll load the dogs up and come right back. We can just bring a tent and make camp at the shed."

"Think he'll let us?"

"Yep. He knows I can take care of myself in the woods."

I hesitated. "Is it, uh—is it safe?"

He looked at me. "You want to get to the bottom of these killings or not?"

Good question. Between Robin and WSI . . .

Back at the shed, Mr. Maxwell was all for Jack's plan.

"I can't afford to lose sheep," he said, frowning —and I suddenly understood why so many farmers were upset. "I've got a big investment in these animals. If I didn't have so much work to do on the farm tomorrow, I'd come with you boys."

But Robin, obviously upset, said, "I just don't think it's Black Betty. I'm not even sure it's a jaguar. Too many things don't add up."

Her father snorted. "What else could it be?" Then his tone softened, and he put his hand on Robin's head. "I know you like animals, baby, but sometimes nature can be cruel."

"If there's a jaguar in these woods, we'll find it," Jack boasted.

It was late afternoon when we got back to the house. Eduardo couldn't go, but he loaned Jack his dogs. We drove back to camp in the old pickup, and just had time to pitch the tent and hang up a lantern before dark. Mrs. Maxwell had packed us plenty of food, so we sat down to eat before beginning the hunt.

"Should be a good night," Jack said, looking up to the starry sky. "No rain to wash the scent away."

Just then thunder rumbled in the distance. Jack groaned, then laughed. "Well, that's Belize for you."

A minute or two later, Jack pointed his half-eaten drumstick into the distance. Down below on the road, the headlights of a vehicle approached slowly, stopping at the gate. The lights went out, doors slammed, and a flashlight approached. Soon Teddy Fever stepped into the lantern light.

"Well well well, if it's not our young hunters," he said with a phony laugh. His two men, machetes strapped to their waists, stood with their arms folded, scowling. "You wouldn't be out after Black Betty, would you now?"

"Why would we be after her?" Jack said.

"Don't play coy with me, lad. Everybody knows she's been on a rampage. I even hear she killed a sheep around here last night."

Jack took another bite of cold chicken. "How'd you know about that?"

The fat man smiled. "Word travels fast in these parts, chappie." He pulled out his wallet. "As you may know, I'm looking for Black Betty myself. But if you should happen to run up on her first—" He held out a bill.

"We don't want your money, Mister," Jack muttered.

Teddy Fever let it drop to the ground. "I'm staying at the Hotel Belmopan," he said. "Room 108." He turned and motioned to his men. "Let's go, boys. We'll let these young nimrods get to work."

18

"That guy's trouble," Jack said as Teddy Fever drove away.

"What do you mean?" I asked.

"I don't know. I just don't trust him. Well—" He stood up and stretched. "Ready for a night's hunt?"

I followed him toward the truck. Halfway there, he turned to me with a puzzled expression. "By the way," he said, "what's a nimrod?"

"I think it means hunter. It's in the Bible."

He thought that over, then climbed into the truck cab. "Let's drive down to the river and turn out near that sheep. Maybe the cat's still somewhere around."

We drove across the bridge. Jack pulled to the roadside and we got out, taking guns and head-lamps. Thunder growled again, closer now, and lightning painted the sky.

"Great," Jack grumbled. "Just what we need—a storm."

"Maybe it'll go around us," I said as he let the dogs out.

"Come on," he told the dogs, heading down the path to the river. "This way."

When we reached the dead sheep, the dogs began to inspect it, but Jack herded them away. "Get away from that! Get out there and find me a jaguar." Reluctantly, the dogs fanned out into the forest.

"Well," Jack said, "I hope it really is Black Betty who killed the sheep, and all the rest of the live-stock, too."

"Why?"

"Because that way, if we get her tonight, the whole problem's solved. The killings stop, the refuge goes ahead. Plus we complete your mission for WSI."

"Yeah, but what if we get Black Betty and the killings continue?"

He spat on the ground. "I look at it this way: If we find a jaguar around here, chances are it's the one that killed Uncle Bill's sheep."

Just then a dog howled, far out in the forest.

"Come on," Jack said, and led the way through the undergrowth.

The other dogs chimed in.

"They've struck a hot trail this time!" Jack said excitedly as we pushed through vines and bushes.

He stopped to listen, one hand up in a signal to keep quiet. The dogs' wild barking was becoming fainter—they were running directly away from us.

"The cat's running!" Jack said. "We'll never catch up. Just listen. Maybe she'll circle back."

The forest flickered with lightning, which made the trees and bushes look spooky. Thunder crashed nearby. I shivered.

"It's fixing to storm big-time," Jack said unhappily. "And that cat is headed straight up into the hills." He glanced at his compass. "Southwest. You know, there's a road over there. If we take the truck we might cut them off."

"But what if the jaguar circles back?" I said.

Jack nodded. "One of us needs to stay here."

I wished I had kept my mouth shut.

"Look," he said, "I'll take the truck. You stay on the sandbar. If you hear the dogs come back this way, keep an eye out. The cat will probably be way ahead of the dogs."

"But what if it starts to rain?" I said, looking nervously at the sky.

"If it gets too bad, go on back to the tent. But this may be our big chance." We reached the sandbar. "This is a good spot," he said. "If I were you I'd cut that light off—save the batteries. You might be out here for a while."

"Uh, Jack?"

"Yeah?" he said impatiently.

I started to ask if I could go with him, but I was afraid he would laugh. "Nothing."

"If you see a jaguar—shoot this time. I'll see you later." He turned away and walked up the path. As I heard the truck drive away, I felt frightened and lonely.

I sat on a log and turned my headlamp off. As much as I feared the darkness, I was more afraid of my batteries running out and leaving me without any light at all.

Rain began to fall, slowly at first, then more heavily. It pattered on my straw hat and ran in streams off the brim, hitting my raincoat. Cold fingers of water pushed down my collar and up my sleeves. *That's enough of this*, I thought. *I'm heading back to camp.*

Just as I stood to leave, lightning lit up the sandbar, revealing a terrifying sight: There, standing by the river with a dead fawn in her mouth, was Black Betty!

I turned on my headlamp and raised my gun —but she was gone.

19

For a moment I wondered whether I had simply imagined the black jaguar. After all, I'd only seen her for a split second.

But no, that vision had been too real—a sight I'd never forget.

I shone my headlamp all around—no cat. What should I do? Run for the tent, or stay put?

Curiosity made me cross the sandbar to look for a footprint. After all, if I had really seen Black Betty, her track should be plain in the sand. I swept my light back and forth.

There it was! And huge—I spread my hand and couldn't cover it.

Shining the light around, I spotted another track—and another! They led along the river's edge in the wet sand, easy to see. Checking to make sure she wasn't nearby, I followed her trail a step at a time.

At the end of the sandbar the prints went up into the jungle. I doubted I could follow them there, but I pushed through the bushes anyway, studying the leaf-covered ground. I saw nothing.

A few steps brought me to a small stream. Sure enough, there was another track, in the mud. She had turned and walked up the streambed. I couldn't believe my luck! I was so excited I didn't even think about being afraid. I knew I was on her trail now. Maybe she didn't even know I was here; maybe she hadn't seen me in the lightning flash.

Why had the dogs taken off for the hills if Black Betty was right here? Maybe she had fooled them and circled back. No, they'd have lost the trail and stopped running. More likely, they were chasing some other cat.

Then another thought struck me: Black Betty hadn't killed Mr. Maxwell's sheep! If she had, why would she be carrying that fawn? She'd have just gone back and eaten the sheep. Robin was right: Black Betty hunted wild game, not livestock.

Thunder rumbled in the distance. The rain seemed to be slacking off; it dripped lazily around me in the leaves. I could hear the storm moving away, like a thunder-giant with lightning spears.

My rubber boots squishing in the mud, I continued up the little creek, spying one footprint after another. Finally the tracks disappeared. I squinted at the bank for a long time before I could see where Black Betty had struck out though the forest.

I'll never be able to track her now, I thought. *The ground's all covered with leaves—no tracks.* And yet, when I aimed my light along the ground, the wet leaves seemed ruffled where she had walked. If I wanted to, I could follow her.

Every nerve in my body screamed to go back to camp. This was crazy! What if she was out there watching me, waiting to pounce? I started to shake. And the gun in my hands didn't make me feel any better. If she wanted to ambush me, I'd never have time to use it.

In fact, what if she was stalking me right now, step by step? Maybe she had gulped down the fawn and was hungry for something bigger.

That's it, I thought. *I'm out of here.* I turned to run back to camp—and instantly tripped and landed face-down in the shallow creek. The cold water was like a slap on my face. *Come out of it, Secret Agent Man*, it seemed to say. *Get a grip.*

I got back to my feet, shook the water out of my face, and shined the light into the jungle. It would be dumb to go back now, I realized. I'd probably never get another chance like this. Besides, Black Betty once had a chance to eat Robin, and she didn't do it.

I began to inch along, peering at the faint trail through the leaves, then swinging the light beam through the jungle around me. Mist smoked among huge leaves and massive tree trunks. I moved the light along the jaguar's trail. Suddenly the beam caught something unusual: the base of a cliff—and a small, dark cave.

Black Betty was in there. I knew it.

My knees felt weak. My heart thumped in my chest. I was afraid to breathe. What if she heard me?

Drip-drip. Water fell from leaves. Then I thought I heard another sound, a crunching noise . . .

Black Betty's teeth crushing the bones of her prey!

I gripped my gun tightly, just in case she changed her mind about eating kids. I didn't want to shoot her—but I didn't want to end up as dessert either.

Slowly, quietly, I began to back away. When I reached the stream, I turned and sloshed quickly down it. I would go back to camp and wait there for Jack. Then I'd tell him that I knew for sure Black Betty wasn't the killer. We'd have to phone Mr. Bugg and ask him what to do.

Unless—maybe Jack's dogs had run down the *real* killer cat. If so, and Jack shot it, our mission would be accomplished!

20

Back at camp, I sat for awhile under the shed in the dark, listening to water drip from leaves. I expected Jack to arrive at any moment with the dogs. But before long I was having a hard time keeping my eyes open, and finally I climbed into the tent and burrowed down in my sleeping bag.

A growl woke me. *Black Betty!* I thought groggily, still mostly asleep. She had stalked me all night and now she was going to eat me for breakfast! I groped for the shotgun—then realized that the "growl" was the sound of Jack's snores. I stared at him and shook my head. But by that time I was wide awake, and I could tell by the light filtering through the tent walls that it was well into the morning. I dressed and went out.

The storm clouds had passed, leaving the sky bright blue. A warm breeze chuckled across the hills. I rummaged in the truck for the food basket and was soon munching on bananas and sweet rolls and sipping from a canteen. Jack climbed out of the tent, sleepy-eyed, hair mussed.

"Find the dogs?" I asked.

He shook his head grumpily. "They crossed the road before I could get there. That cat probably led them clear to Guatemala."

"So what's next, then?"

He stretched and began peeling a banana. "I'll go back to where they crossed and blow the horn. They'll come back." He shook his head. "Eventually."

"Never saw the jaguar, huh?"

He scowled, biting into the fruit. "Nothing."

I grinned. "I did."

He raised his eyebrows. "You kidding?"

"Nope. I saw Black Betty."

"But the dogs . . ."

"Must have been chasing another jaguar. I was down there by the sandbar when Black Betty came by."

Jack nodded grimly. "Figures. Came back to get the sheep."

I shook my head, smiling. "Wrong, Jack. She had a fawn in her mouth. She never even went near the sheep."

"A fawn? Are you sure?"

I nodded.

"Didn't go near the sheep?" he persisted.

"Didn't act like she even knew it was there."

Still trying to wake up, he combed his hair with his fingers and scratched himself vigorously through his shirt. He peeled another banana. "Then we know she's not the one doing the killing. Must be that other one, the one the dogs chased."

I started to tell him about finding the lair, but decided not to. Jack was such a devoted hunter he might want to ambush her anyway. No, I wouldn't risk it.

"Look," he said, eating a roll, "I'm going to drive around and blow the horn for the dogs. You mind taking down the tent and getting everything ready to go? If the dogs don't show up in a couple hours, I'll come back and get you. Then we'll ride around and look some more, I guess."

"All right."

As he drove away, I began breaking camp. I rolled up the sleeping bags, took down the tent, and stacked everything under the shed. Then I sat in a folding chair and watched Mr. Maxwell's sheep graze peacefully in the grass.

I yawned. A fly buzzed around my head. When it lit on my nose I swatted at it. Closing my eyes, I listened to the munch of grazing sheep, the drone of insects, the call of distant birds.

I was just drifting off when I heard a motor. A dark blue jeep pulled up to the gate below, a license plate reading "Belmopan Car Rental." Hmmm.

The doors opened; five people got out. Robin and Mr. Lee—what were they doing here, and in a strange vehicle?

They walked toward me, accompanied by a tall, dark-haired man, a brown-haired boy and a girl with long, honey-blond hair.

The Stirlings!

21

"We flew in last night," Erik K. explained, after we'd greeted each other. "Dad rented a jeep and we drove down to the Maxwells' farm."

"Eric, why didn't you *tell* me you were a secret agent?" Robin asked.

I looked at Dr. Stirling, who nodded. "It's all right, Eric C.," he said. "I filled the Maxwells in on the situation. I figured we might need their help."

"I thought there might be more to this boy than meets the eye," said Mr. Lee, putting a hand on my shoulder. "I've known a secret agent or two in my time, but never one quite so young."

He and Dr. Stirling sat in the two folding chairs while the rest of us sat on the ground.

"When we got your message I called WSI," Dr. Stirling told me.

"What did Mr. Bugg say?"

"Miss Spice was back from vacation, I'm happy to say, and she said do *not* kill Black Betty."

"Boy, am I glad to hear that," I breathed.

"I don't understand why WSI wanted her killed in the first place," Robin said.

"Me either," Sharon said, rolling her eyes.

"Well, killing Black Betty was Mr. Bugg's idea," Dr. Stirling said. "He hoped to get rid of the cat so the problem would fade away quietly. I think we all agree his idea wasn't the best one."

"Aren't you glad you didn't shoot Black Betty that night?" Robin whispered to me.

"Thanks to you," I said.

"Wait'll you hear Dad's idea," Sharon said.

"What is it, Dr. Stirling?" I asked.

"I talked to the zoo officials, and they agreed that I should come down and try to capture Black Betty alive and take her back."

"All right!" I said.

Robin grinned, but then looked sad. "I'm glad she won't be shot, but I'll miss her."

"I'm sure you would, Robin," Dr. Stirling said sympathetically. "But for Black Betty's own good we have to take her out of Belize—she's become too infamous. There will always be hunters after her, even if we can prove she wasn't the one doing the killings. There's been too much negative publicity."

"But what about the *real* killer jaguar?" Erik K. asked. "Won't the killings continue?"

Dr. Stirling sighed. "We're hoping Jack can succeed in getting it."

Robin shook her head. "I don't think it's a jaguar at all."

"The girl may be right," Mr. Lee said, nodding. "I've never heard of a jaguar killing a cow a night. Also, Robin told me about that sheep, lying in plain sight. That's not like a jaguar either. They tend to hide their prey after they kill it."

"That's true," Dr. Stirling said.

"Is the sheep around here?" Erik K. asked.

I pointed. "Right down the road."

"Let's go take a look," Dr. Stirling said, rising. "Then I've got to run into Belmopan to meet with government officials. Mr. Lee has agreed to show me around."

"Dad, why don't you show Eric C. the gun?" Erik K. asked as we reached the jeep.

"All right." Dr. Stirling opened the back to reveal a long black case. Inside lay a rifle with a scope and a number of unusual "bullets" beside it.

"Those look like syringes," I said.

"That's what he plans to shoot Black Betty with," Sharon said. "Tranquilizer darts."

"Neat!" I said.

As we walked down the road, I told them about last night's hunt, and about trailing Black Betty to her den. "Maybe she's still in there," I said. "Do you think we should try to sneak up on her right now?"

"Unfortunately, I shouldn't do anything until I talk with government officials," Dr. Stirling said. "The director of the zoo has already talked with them on the phone, but I need to confirm the agreement and get some papers signed. Besides, it's unlikely she would still be in her den. Jaguars don't usually stay in one place long."

"We'll just have to get Jack to put his dogs on her trail," Robin said—for the first time ever sounding enthusiastic about a hunt.

We crossed the bridge and stepped down the path. "There's the sheep," I said.

A cloud of flies rose from the carcass as we approached. "Yuck!" Erik said, wrinkling his nose at the stink.

"You kids stay there if you like," Dr. Stirling said. "I'll take a closer look."

But Erik, Sharon, and Mr. Lee all followed him, leaving Robin and me together on the path. She slipped her hand into mine and gave it a squeeze.

"I'm so excited," she whispered, her eyes glowing. "Black Betty's going to live!"

"Don't forget, Teddy Fever's still hunting her," I said.

She nodded, then released my hand quickly as the others turned back toward us.

Dr. Stirling looked puzzled. "That's highly un-usual for a jaguar kill," he said.

"You mean because it's not hidden?" Robin asked.

"Not just that. There are no wounds on the lower body. A cat usually slashes with its hind feet as it kills."

"How about dogs?" Erik asked.

His father shook his head. "They would have ripped the intestines out, first thing. I could almost believe a bear did it, with that clean cut on the throat like a claw would make, but of course there aren't any bears around here."

"I've got it," Mr. Lee said, holding up a finger. "I know what did it."

We stared expectantly.

"A boa constrictor."

"Then why didn't it eat the sheep?" I asked.

"Someone probably scared it off before it got a chance."

Dr. Stirling shook his head. "With all due respect, I've never heard of a boa constrictor going for the throat."

"Ah! But I daresay you don't know boa constric-tors like I do," Mr. Lee said, and Robin and I grinned at each other. "Have I told you about the time I personally was attacked by one, Dr. Stirling?"

The veterinarian glanced at his watch. "Why don't you tell me on the way to Belmopan, Mr. Lee? We need to get a move on if I'm going to get this paperwork done. You kids stay around here. We'll be back as soon as possible."

"Good luck, Dad," Sharon called as the two men walked toward the jeep.

22

"How about taking us to see the cave, Eric C.?" Sharon asked.

"What's all this 'Eric C.' business?" Robin said, turning to me. "I thought your last name started with an S."

The rest of us laughed. "It's a long story," I said. "But here's the short version: His name is Erik Stirling —E-r-i-k S-t-i-r-l-i-n-g—and mine is Eric Sterling— E-r-i-c S-t-e-r-l-i-n-g."

"To avoid confusion, we call him Eric C. and my brother Erik K.," Sharon said.

"Oh," Robin said. "Weird."

"Well, come on, let's go see the cave," Erik said.

"Do you think we should?" Sharon asked. "What if Black Betty's still there and we scare her off?"

"You heard what Dad said," her brother argued. "She's probably not there. Besides, we'll be real quiet."

I looked at Robin. "What do you think?"

She shrugged and grinned. "Let's go."

At the river I scouted around for the tracks I had seen last night. "There's one," I said. "It's not fresh anymore, but you can still make it out."

"Wow, that's big!" Erik said.

I led them along the sandbar and up into the jungle to the little stream. "Too bad you guys don't have rubber boots on like Robin and me," I said, stepping into the squishy mud.

"Yucky," said Sharon, picking her way carefully in white tennis shoes.

"See those tracks?" I whispered. "They're easy to follow in the mud, but it's not that easy once she leaves this stream."

We continued up the creek until the prints disappeared. I put my finger to my lips, and we tiptoed silently into the forest. At last I made out the cliff and the cave. I stopped and pointed. My friends nodded.

Robin put her lips to my ear. "That's about the same size as the den at my place."

"Yeah," I whispered. "I wonder how many dens she's got?"

"I'll bet she's got a bunch."

Erik leaned toward me. "Can we get any closer?" he whispered.

"Probably not a good idea—you know, just in case she's in there."

"What if we get down on our hands and knees and crawl?"

I looked at Robin and Sharon. They nodded. We all dropped to the ground and began inching along. I strained to listen for cat noises—breathing, purring, eating. But suddenly I heard a different sound—dogs!

"Oh, no!" Robin gasped. "It's Jack!"

"What should we do?" Erik asked.

"We've got to warn him not to shoot her," I whispered. "Man, I wish your dad was here."

Sharon said, "These dogs'll spook the jaguar for sure."

"If she's in there," I added.

As the dogs neared, we watched the mouth of the cave—just in case.

It happened so fast we could hardly see it—a black shadow slipped out of the hole and vanished into the forest.

"That was her!" Sharon said excitedly. "That was Black Betty—wasn't it?"

"That was her, all right," Robin said, sounding worried.

We rose to our feet just as a pack of hunting dogs raced past, giving us barely a glance as they chased after their prey.

"Hey, those aren't Jack's dogs," I said.

"Whose are they, then?" Robin asked.

Heavy footsteps clomped toward us through the underbrush. In a few moments, the bushes parted and out waddled Teddy Fever—red-faced, sweating heavily, and panting. As usual he wore his safari suit, with a large hunting knife strapped to his belt and a rifle in his hands.

"That's Teddy Fever!" I whispered to Robin.

The man scowled when he saw us. "What are you kids doing out here?" he said grumpily, mopping his face with a handkerchief.

Robin stepped toward him. "If you're hunting Black Betty, she's not the one who's been killing livestock!"

"The devil she isn't! She's the one and I'm going to get her. Listen!" He nodded. "The dogs have got her treed right now."

"Wait!" Robin said. "She's innocent, really!"

Ignoring us, Teddy Fever brushed past.

"Come on! We've got to stop him!" Robin urged.

We hurried after the fat hunter. As we jogged around a thicket, we saw a pack of dogs barking wildly at the base of a tree. Above them, in the branches, easy to see in daylight, was Black Betty, looking angry and scared.

Standing under the tree, Teddy Fever raised his rifle and aimed.

"No!" Robin screamed, rushing toward him. "Please don't shoot!"

23

Suddenly Teddy Fever lowered his gun and swatted his neck. "Ouch! Blasted insects!" He started to raise his gun again but it slipped from his fingers. He staggered sideways and fell to the ground.

Hearing a noise behind us, we whirled around —and saw Dr. Stirling, reloading his tranquilizer gun. Behind him stood Mr. Lee.

"Good shot, Dad!" Erik K. said.

Dr. Stirling nodded grimly. "I figure that gentleman weighs at least as much as a jaguar, so the dosage should have been just about right."

"How did you get back so soon?" Sharon asked.

"He flagged us down on the road. First he asked if we'd seen a couple of boys with hunting dogs, then if we knew anything about Black Betty."

"I recognized him from his picture in the papers," Mr. Lee added.

"I didn't like the idea of his hunting up here near you kids," Dr. Stirling said, "so we circled back and followed him."

"Thank heavens!" Robin said.

"Now we've got another little task." He motioned to the tree.

"What about the signatures you need?" Sharon asked.

"I'll just have to take care of that later. We can't pass up an opportunity like this."

Stepping near the tree, he raised the rifle. But Robin touched his elbow and whispered something to him. Dr. Stirling looked at me and nodded. Then he offered me the rifle. "You do it, Eric C."

"Me? But why?"

"You've done all the work on this case. I think it's right that you finish it." He chuckled. "Plus, after your lessons from Mr. Bugg, you're probably a better shot than I am."

"No way." But I took the gun. Its wooden stock felt glossy and smooth in my hands.

Turning to the tree, I raised the rifle and peered through the scope, sighting Black Betty in the crosshairs. The whole world fell silent as her eyes seemed to fasten on me, staring straight into my soul.

I hoped she understood that I was her friend, that I was doing this to help her. Feeling the slick curve of the trigger under my finger, I squeezed.

Poof! The silver dart stuck in Black Betty's neck. She didn't even seem to notice. But in a few moments she began to appear sleepy. Picking her way down the tree, she slid to the ground, unconscious.

In an instant the pack of dogs was on her, growling and biting. We raced into the middle of them, kicking, shouting, and pulling. The hounds backed off and darted into the woods, watching from a distance.

"No serious damage," Dr. Stirling said, examining the cat. He pulled a nylon muzzle from his hip pocket and slipped it over Black Betty's mouth. "I expect she'll be out for some time, but there's no sense in taking chances."

The rest of us clustered around. "She's a beauty," Mr. Lee said.

Black Betty was huge, with massive paws and a long, thick tail. Though her fur was very dark, I could still make out her spots.

Robin and I dropped to our knees and stroked the jaguar's glossy, thick pelt. Sharon examined her eyes, then her ears. "No ticks," she said.

Erik squeezed the cat's upper legs. "Man, feel those muscles!"

"Erik K., I need you to come with me to the car to get the stretcher and foot covers," Dr. Stirling said.

"What about him?" Sharon asked, pointing to Teddy Fever, who lay motionless in the leaves.

Dr. Stirling knelt beside the fat man and checked his pulse. "He's fine," he said. "He'll come to in a little while. I guess I'd better unload his gun, in case he gets any crazy ideas."

"I know how to do it," I said. Ejecting a bullet from the chamber and removing the clip, I handed them to Dr. Stirling. Then, to be on the safe side, I pulled Teddy Fever's hunting knife from its leather sheath.

"Can I see that?" Erik asked.

I handed it to him.

He bounced it lightly in his palm. "One of these days I'm going to learn how to throw a knife." Then he stared at it more closely. "Something on the blade. Dried blood or something."

Dr. Stirling looked up, interested. "I'd like to take a look." Erik passed it handle-first to his father, who squinted at the steel. "Yes, it is dried blood. Nothing odd about a hunter having dried blood on his knife, of course. Still . . ."

"The sheep?" Robin said, arching her eyebrows.

"Just what I was thinking," Dr. Stirling said quietly.

We all stared at Teddy Fever, who began to snore.

"But why?" I asked.

Hearing footsteps, we saw Teddy Fever's two helpers approaching through the jungle.

"What happen to de boss mon?" one of them asked, frowning.

Then they saw the jaguar.

"Black Betty!" the other gasped. They stared at Dr. Stirling and his rifle. "Did you kill 'er, sir?"

"Shoot her, yes. Kill her, no." Holding up the knife, Dr. Stirling stared at the pair suspiciously. "Do you have any idea why he would want to kill livestock with this?"

They glanced at each other nervously.

"I'd advise you to talk," Dr. Stirling said. "I suspect your boss is in big trouble. He's not hurt, by the way, just unconscious, like the cat. Now, if you don't want to be in trouble too, you'd be well advised to tell me what you know."

"Boss mon tell ever'body Black Betty kill all de cattle and sheep," one of the men stammered. "He want to scare de people so de gov-men' no set up dat dere jaguar refuge."

"But why?" Robin asked.

"He want de land for himself," said the other man. "He want to start a big tourist resort. He figure if de gov-men' can't make jaguar refuge, dey sell de land cheap-cheap."

His friend nodded. "He tell all de newspaper dat Black Betty killin' de cattle. He say jaguar refuge no good. All de time he hopin' he can buy de land from de gov-men' and make lots o' money."

Dr. Stirling nodded. "So jaguars aren't responsible for the killings."

"Dat's right."

I snapped my fingers. "*That's* how Teddy Fever knew the sheep had been killed that day. He'd killed it himself, and left it by the path so someone would see it and blame the jaguar."

"You fellows stick around," Dr. Stirling said to the men. "I'm sure you'll be called on to testify. Don't worry, I'll tell the police you've cooperated. As for your boss—" He shook his head. "I'm afraid he's in hot water."

The men nodded as if they had expected something like this to happen sooner or later.

"Come on, Erik K.," Dr. Stirling said. "We'll be back in a few minutes," he told the rest of us.

We sat down to wait. The two men leaned against trees, arms folded, looking worried. A fly buzzed around Teddy Fever's face, but he didn't move.

Mr. Lee, his legs stretched out on the ground and his back against a tree, yawned loudly. "I do believe it's just about my nap time," he said, closing his eyes. His head nodded a time or two, then his chin rested on his chest as he dozed.

Suddenly we heard a low growl. Sharon, Robin, and I looked first at each other, then at the jaguar.

Black Betty was waking up!

24

We jumped to our feet. The cat stirred in the leaves, struggling to raise her head. Teddy Fever's helpers began backing away.

"Wait!" Sharon said. "Everyone stay still."

She approached the jaguar cautiously. Staring at her through half-lidded eyes, the big cat tried to rise again, but seemed to have no control over her body. Sharon put her hands on the jaguar's head and began to massage its temples while making a deep purring noise. Slowly the animal lay back down, closed her eyes, and seemed to sleep.

The two men stared at Sharon in awe. "How you do dat?" one asked.

Sharon grinned. "I just took a course in lion taming."

"That's incredible!" Robin said.

Mr. Lee smacked his lips and opened his eyes. "Did somebody call me?"

Everyone laughed. "Glad everyone seems to be having a good time," Dr. Stirling said with a grin as he and Erik K. returned. Dr. Stirling covered the cat's paws with nylon pads, and with the men's help loaded her onto a canvas stretcher. With Dr. Stirling, Erik K., and the two men carrying the jaguar, we all headed back to the road. The rental jeep was parked next to Teddy Fever's camouflaged safari truck.

"Let's put her in the back of the truck," Dr. Stirling said. "Mr. Lee, I'm going to rely on you to take the jeep to town and get the police. I'll ask these two gentlemen to go with me to get this cat in a cage before she comes to."

Just then a pickup truck came rumbling up the road—Jack! He stopped beside us and stared in wonder at the black jaguar lying in the back of Teddy Fever's truck. Jack's dogs milled around in their box, barking uneasily.

"You got her!" he said in astonishment.

We laughed. "It's a long story, cousin," Robin said.

"Let's just say it's mission accomplished," I added.

"But why'd you kill her, after everything we found out?"

"We didn't," I said. "We shot her with a tranquilizer dart. Don't worry, we'll explain everything. You found the dogs, I see."

"Yeah, they finally showed up. I was just coming to get you."

"You kids can go on back to the Maxwells' farm," Dr. Stirling told us. "Mr. Lee and I will take care of everything from here. We'll see you tonight."

Robin and I climbed into the cab of Jack's pickup while Erik K. and Sharon got in back.

"Let's go get the camping equipment," Jack said, putting the vehicle in gear, "and then I want to hear everything."

Robin and I looked at each other and grinned.

✳✳✳

That night Dr. Stirling and Mr. Lee returned to the Maxwell's farm just in time for supper.

"This has been one of the busiest days I remember," Dr. Stirling said, easing himself wearily into his chair at the table.

"Is Black Betty okay?" Robin asked.

"She's in great shape. In fact—" He glanced at his watch. "She should be on her way to the States right about now. Zoo officials will meet her at the airport and take her to her new home."

"What about Teddy Fever?" Jack asked.

Dr. Stirling smiled wryly. "Behind bars. With the testimony of his own two men, he doesn't have a defense. We saw to it that the newspaper learned about his scheme too."

"There'll be some angry farmers around here when they find out what that scoundrel has done,"

Mr. Maxwell said. "At the very least, he'll pay dearly for the livestock he's killed."

Mr. Lee nodded. "He'll be lucky if they don't hang him. Why, I remember a gang of outlaws back in 1959 . . ."

***

That night after supper, Robin and I stepped out onto the back porch.

"I'm sure going to miss this place," I said.

"I'm going to miss you, too."

She took my hand. I glanced around to make sure no one was watching.

"Couldn't you stay on and help us pick cucumbers or something?" Robin asked.

"I wish. But Dr. Stirling said we have to leave in the morning."

"Maybe you could join the 4-H and come back as a *real* exchange student." She giggled.

"That'd be neat. Then you could show me more of the farm and everything." I peeked over my shoulder, afraid someone would come outside suddenly and see us holding hands.

"There's lots more to see," she said. Then her voice became almost a whisper. "I've never met a real secret agent before."

"Oh, all that stuff doesn't really mean anything. Actually, they got me by mistake. Kind of. I mean, I'm just an ordinary kid."

"Not to me you're not, Eric."

She leaned over to kiss me just as I was looking around, and her kiss landed right on my lips. My eyes flew open wide—I was so surprised I stumbled backward, and I'd have fallen right off the porch if Robin hadn't held me tightly by the hand.

"Wow! Thanks," I said, recovering my balance.

"Let's see, you saved me from a snake, I saved you from falling off the truck, and now I kept you from falling off the porch." In the darkness I saw her smile. "I'd say you owe me one."

I felt my hands grow sweaty as she stepped in close for another kiss. I wanted to run, I wanted to hide—but hey, a guy's got to pay his debts.

25

"So how was your vacation, Miss Spice?" Erik K. asked.

The three of us sat in her office sipping pineapple juice and munching macadamia nuts, which she had brought back from Hawaii.

"Wonderful!" she said. "Like my tan?"

"Looks great," Sharon said.

"You kids did a great job in my absence." She lowered her voice. "This is between you and me, but if I had been here I would have handled things a bit differently."

"I knew it," I said, nodding.

"As soon as I heard you'd been told to kill the jaguar, I was afraid there would be problems," she said. "We should have talked to the zoo to start with about tranquilizing Black Betty and bringing her back."

"But Mr. Bugg was a nice guy—and he's a great gun instructor," I said.

"Oh, he's a fine man," Miss Spice said quickly. "He had a hard decision to make, and he made it. Plus, he used to be a professional hunting guide, so he certainly saw no problem in killing one jaguar to save many. I'm just happy we didn't have to kill *any*."

"Me too!" Sharon said.

Miss Spice pulled several newspapers from a drawer and passed them across the desk to us.

"'Man arrested for livestock killings,'" Sharon read.

"'Black jaguar not to blame, officials say,'" Erik read.

"'Government to discuss new jaguar refuge,'" I read.

Miss Spice smiled. "I'm sorry you had to do this one by yourself, Eric C., but it looks like you handled it well."

"Thanks, but if Erik K. and Sharon and their dad hadn't shown up, I think Teddy Fever would have shot Black Betty and probably gotten away with his whole rotten scheme," I said.

"Oh, you and Robin would have stopped him somehow," Sharon said. "You two had already figured out that Black Betty wasn't killing the livestock."

At the mention of Robin's name, I felt my face go hot.

"Well, I'll bet Eric C. has had his fill of jungles and jaguars," Miss Spice said.